DEDICATION

Growing up every girl's fantasy was to find a love like we read about or see on Tv. The type of love that makes your soul set fire. The type of love when you stare into their eyes, your insides melt. That unconditional love. That type of love is rare and damn near don't exist, but on January 31, 2011 I found that love. After fighting for hours and preparing myself for the worst, a girl was born. I didn't know how special she would be to me, nor did I know what being her mother would entail. After looking in her eyes, I knew then that no matter what I went through in this world, I had found someone who would love me with all of their being. I knew then I would move mountains, swim a river, and go through any storm to protect her. She would always know what it's like to be loved beyond reason. I have been doing that every day since birth and I will continue to do just that. Miracle Monet Riley mommy loves you baby to the moon and back, forever and a day, and my heart will always beat for you.

1

ACKNOWLEDGEMENTS

To everyone that has downloaded, shared, read, and loved a book by Latoya Nicole I thank you from the bottom of my heart. You are the reason I am here and giving my best. Keep pushing us authors to be better. I love you…

To my granny Bessie Joan, happy bday I love you and you're the reason I fight the way I do. You taught us to never give up on our dreams and I'm fighting and pushing until I hit that goal. Wish I was there to celebrate with you, but know I love you with all of my heart.

To my girls my admin team, you are awesome and I could never thank you enough. ZaTasha, Kb Cole, Ash, Paris, Panda, Juanita, Dawn, Amber if you rocking I'm rolling. I love yall.

Bitch Squad, I love yall and thank you for making every day a great one. Keep pushing each other to be better. SQUUAADD.

To my test reader ZaTasha, you are the freaking best. I love you and don't ever forget it.

To my family and friends

You been there since the beginning and I appreciate what you saw in me from the jump. You believed in me at times I didn't believe in myself. Keep being that force that is pushing me to be great. I love yall.

Book 10 let's go.

LOVE AND WAR 4

A GANGSTA'S LAST RIDE

LATOYA NICOLE

PROLOGUE

DREA...

Walking through the grocery store, I thought about how far we had come. Everything was going great in all of our lives. Looking down at Spark, I smiled as she reached for the lighter fluid.

"No baby, we don't play with that." Looking up at me with her bright gray eyes, she smiled. I swear this baby was only a year old and I can tell she was going to be just like her daddy. She was attracted to anything with a flame and I tried my best to keep her away from the shit. Since she was sitting in the buggy, I stepped a couple feet away to get her some grapes. Thinking she needed to eat more fruit, I grabbed some bananas. Turning around, I placed the items in the cart.

"What the fuck. Spark. Spark baby where are you?" Not wanting to think the worse, I walked around the store praying she climbed out of the buggy. Starting to panic, I stopped anybody walking by.

"Excuse me, have you seen a little girl? She has grey eyes, curly hair, and she has on all pink."

"No I'm sorry." Fuck, Blaze was about to kill me. Running to the front, I had the manager say it over the loud speaker.

"If anybody sees a little girl wearing all pink by herself, please bring her to the front desk."

"Can you give them her description?"

"Ma'am, I'm sure that there is only one baby walking around by their self." Ready to slap his ass, I let him be great and took off running around the store to look for her. The more time that passed, the more tears fell down my face. Reality was starting to set in, my baby was not in this store.

"Can the mother of the missing child please come to the front desk." When I heard that over the loud speaker, I took off running towards the front. Thank God they found her. When I got to the desk, I didn't see her and I didn't understand what the fuck was going on.

"One of our staff members said they saw a man carrying her out of the store and put her into a van. Was it her father? Do you need us to call the police?" Ignoring his questions, I took off running to the parking lot. Her shoe was laying by the curb and I broke down. Grabbing my phone, I made the call I never thought I would have to make.

"Baby, get to Jewels right now."

"What's wrong Drea?"

"Somebody kidnapped Spark."

"If my baby not there by the time I make it, you gone be one dead hoe." Knowing I didn't want to face Blaze's wrath, I went back in the store and prayed the man saw the wrong baby.

CHAPTER 1- BLAZE

"Come here daddy's baby. Walk to daddy." Spark made it halfway and then dropped down to crawl. As soon as she got over to me, she reached for the lighter in my hand. "Let it go, I told you not to play with daddy's toy."

"Why the hell are you walking around carrying that shit anyway? We have a toddler, you can't have that shit around."

"Girl if you don't get your ass out my face and take your ass somewhere and wash that pussy. You done had that shit on since yesterday, I know that cat hot. I mean if you want a hot pussy I can help you out." Flicking my Bic, she rolled her eyes and walked away. "Your ass better be getting in that shower."

"Blaze don't do that, you know damn well I been getting shit ready for this get together. You ain't helped me with shit."

"So you saying because you been cooking, you couldn't wash that hot pocket? Girl if you don't get your nasty ass out my face and go wash your ass."

"Whatever asshole, I'm going." Putting my lighter away, I continued to play with my angel. I couldn't believe baby girl was one. A nigga ain't felt real love until they have a child.

"Da Da, juice."

"You thirsty ma ma? Hold on." Walking in the kitchen, I grabbed her cup and poured her some juice. When I got back in the front room, it was a big ass flame in the fire place.

"DREA!! COME HERE HURRY UP." Drea came running down the stairs and damn near bust her shit she was running so fast.

"Oh my God, what happened." Tearing up, I had to gather my thoughts.

"She threw her blanket in the fire place. That shit touched a nigga heart. She gone be just like a nigga."

"Have you lost your damn mind? Your ass happy because our one year old in here playing with fire."

"You damn right. At least now I know she mine. Don't look at me like that. You know that pussy got some miles on it while I was dead."

"You have issues. Give me my damn baby. She gone be done set the whole house on fire and your dumb ass will stand there proud and happy." She grabbed Spark and I slapped her on the ass.

"Your lips getting looser than your pussy. I retired baby, but I still got my Bic. I'm trying to let you be great, but your ass determined to feel this heat."

"You set me on fire again, you gone feel a divorce."

"Divorce deez nuts." Smacking her lips, she went back upstairs. Heading in the kitchen, I started grabbing the food and taking it outside. She did all the sides and I was supposed to do the meat. Pouring the charcoal in, I covered it in lighter fluid. As soon as I flicked my Bic, I started thinking about all the good times I had over my life with this mother fucker. It was hard for me to walk away, but I did if for my family. Not realizing I was standing there just looking at the flame in my hand, Drea brought me out of my thoughts.

"Baby are you happy? Do you miss the streets?" Turning to face her, I could see the worry in her eyes.

"Sometimes. The rush we got from hitting those banks or killing people was like no other. Some nights I think about sneaking out and finding somebody and setting they ass on fire. That fire to flesh smell, man I miss that shit. But I would walk away ten thousand times for my family. I'm happy, a nigga just miss the shit sometime."

"That's some sick shit baby." She shook her head at me as she laughed.

"The fact that I had to tell your ass more than once to go wash your ass is sick. The fucked up part is, you still ain't got in that mother fucker. Let me find out you done tricked me and I done married a mother fucker that take hoe baths with her leg kicked up on the sink."

"I hate your ass." Laughing, I turned around and flicked my Bic again. Placing the fire to the Charcoal, that mother fucker shot up and damn near took a nigga's fade clean off. I could smell burning, so I know that shit got me. My dumb ass tried to light the grill with a lil ass lighter.

"That's what the fuck you get. God don't like ugly."

"I bet he hate funky bitches more. For real bae, this is starting to get weird. You got ten seconds to get your ass in the house and wash your ass or I'm gone sterilize that mother fucker."

"Sterilize it?"

"You know when you boil something it's sterilized. I'm about to cook your shit. My dick hard as fuck and I can't even ask for no damn pussy. Shit smelling like do not disturb."

"Bye Blaze." She walked off and I lit the grill the right way and started the meat. Hearing the doorbell, I walked through the house and answered the door.

"Hello sir, I have something for you." Looking at the envelope, I knew I hadn't ordered shit. Seeing it was no name or address on it, I turned that shit down.

"Naw bruh, I'm straight. Take that shit back where you got it."

"It's just a…"

"Nigga are you deaf or slow? I said I don't want that shit." Seeing he still had no intentions to leave, I reached in my pocket and grabbed my lighter.

"I know you don't know me cus if you did, you wouldn't be standing in front of me looking like Lionel Richie. You got so many chemicals in your hair, that fire would spread quick. Now I asked you to get the fuck off my porch. You need to leave before I forget I'm retired." He looked at me as if he was trying to see if I was serious. As soon as I flicked my Bic, he took off down the driveway. Smart man. Closing the door. I headed back towards the kitchen when the doorbell rang again. This nigga had me fucked up. Swinging the door open, I went the fuck off.

"What the fuck did I say?" Seeing my mama and the pastor standing there, I calmed down.

"Nigga if you don't watch your damn mouth. Who raised your ass. You so damn disrespectful." Me and the pastor looked at each other and bust out laughing. My mama didn't even realize she cursed worse than I did.

"Pastor when you step in here, just know. I ain't shit and as you already know my mama ain't either. Just pray for me."

"Son, be careful what you ask for. I believe God has a plan for your life."

"Hold the fuck on. Ain't gone be no preaching in my shit. I had to listen to your long winded ass at the wedding. Not today mother fucker, not today. Ma what the fuck you doing with him anyway?"

"Nigga I said watch your mouth. Damn. You trying to run my damn man away." The Pastor started blushing and I was ready to knock his ass out.

"What's your name Pastor?"

"Devon."

"Devon, if you hurt my mama, I'm gone burn you so bad you gone think your ass done went to Hell. Are we clear?" Clearing his throat, he started to look nervous.

"Yes, we are clear."

"Good, now leave all that Holy shit on the porch. We about to turn the fuck up and act a whole ass out here today. I don't need you trying to pray for our souls." Moving out the way, I finally let them in the house.

"Nigga move out the damn way. Shit I'm hungry. Is the food done."

"Naw ma, I just started the meat."

"Go change your clothes, I got it. The shit better not be burnt either."

"You know what the fuck my name is. If I don't know shit else, I know fire."

"Then why the fuck you sitting here looking like a damn rapist with alopecia in the eyebrows?" Running to the mirror, I looked and the damn fire took my eyebrows off.

"Ain't this a bitch."

"Get your blank ass on. I got the meat. Nigga sitting there looking like nothing. Ain't shit on this nigga face." Her and Devon started laughing until I looked at his ass. He shut up quick.

"You catch on fast Devon. I'll set your damn throat on fire and have your ass preaching smoke on Sunday. Yall got me fucked up." Heading up the stairs, I prayed Drea could help me. My brothers was gone let my ass have it if they saw me like this. My mama called my ass blank, I'm gone get her ass back. She got me fucked up.

CHAPTER 2- BABY FACE

"Baby Tsunami need some attention. Where the fuck you at?" When she didn't respond, I got up and walked around looking for her. Stepping in baby Zaria's room, Juicy was lying next to the crib knocked out. This baby was wearing our ass out. We hardly ever had time for each other anymore. I swear I love my girl to death, but all her spoiled ass does is cry. Her lil ass gone be an attention seeker. If she even thinks a mother fucker not paying her attention she starts crying and shit. She won't sleep at night and she cries all during the damn day. I don't know how Juicy got her ass sleep now, but I was about to use that shit to my advantage to get my dick sucked. Walking over to Juicy, I pulled Tsunami out and pushed against her lips. When she didn't wake up, I slapped her ass in the face with that big mother fucker.

"What the fuck." As soon as she screamed that shit, the baby started crying.

"Damn Juicy, this was our first moment to ourselves."

"Nigga you the one came in here slapping a bitch with your third leg." Bending down to get the baby, she started rocking and I tried to speak in a calm tone.

"When the baby went to sleep, why the fuck didn't you come find me? You know we don't got time for shit."

"Your hand works. Use that shit."

"I shouldn't have to when I got a wife at home. This is starting to get ridiculous. A nigga ain't had no sex in three fucking months." She shrugged her shoulders and walked away. Rubbing my hand down my face, I was getting frustrated. Don't get me wrong, being a father was the best thing in the fucking world. But the shit that comes with it was stressing a nigga out. It's like the old Juicy was gone. My ass trying to be faithful, but she making this shit hard. How long does she expect a nigga like me to go without sex? Walking out of the nursery, I went in our room and prayed the baby was sleep. When I saw that she was, I got excited as hell.

"Come on, let's get a quickie in before she wakes up."

"I don't feel like it damn. Can a bitch get a break?"

"This ain't no fucking break, this a damn retirement. What the fuck you need a break from? I'm not understanding."

"FROM YOU. All you do is crowd me and beg for sex. Damn can a bitch breathe."

"This is why niggas cheat. I ain't never seen a mother fucker have to beg for sex from his own damn wife."

"Go cheat then, it ain't like you never done it before. Get the fuck out of my face." Walking up to her, I grabbed her around her throat.

"You feeling yourself too much. Don't forget who the fuck I am." Letting her neck go, I walked away to go get in the shower. She started crying and I had no fucks to give. Slamming the bathroom door, I hope the baby woke up on her goofy ass.

"I fucking hate you."

"Touché bitch. Touché." I yelled through the door. Stepping in the water, I was starting to think I made a mistake. This was not how my life was supposed to be going. Retiring from the streets was a decision we made because we were trying to be family men. Outside of my daughter, I was feeling like this bitch

18

can leave. Grabbing my body wash, I started stroking my dick. Seeing him come to life, all I wanted to do was put him in some pussy. Slowly stroking my shit, I closed my eyes and imagined me being balls deep. By it being so long since I had some pussy, my nut started rising up quick. Fuck. This mother fucker was cumming hard and strong. The shit shot out of me so hard, my knees got weak. When the feeling came back in my legs, I washed my ass and got the fuck out. Walking out the bathroom, I saw her laying in the bed sleep. I started to slap the shit out of her ass. Nigga thirty years old and beating his meat. Looking at the clock, I knew it was time to start getting ready for the cook out. Deciding to be petty, I got dressed and left her ass. Jumping in my Hummer, I headed over to Blaze's house.

As soon as I walked in the door, all of my troubles left my mind. I loved being around my brothers. We had a bond like no other. These niggas kept me laughing. Shadow and Quick hadn't made it yet, but I saw my mama was here. Leaning down to give her a kiss, I side eyed the pastor. The fuck was he doing here?

"Ma, I thought you said you wasn't on that shit?"

"Nigga don't question me. A bitch need some dick, why not get some Holy penis dipped off in me? Shid I get a nut and a blessing at the same time."

"You nasty as hell and that ain't how that shit work. I hope your ass shaved."

"Don't worry about it bitch, I know somebody that like it." Laughing as she tried to mimic Ms. Pearly, I walked away and grabbed me a drink.

"What up nigga? Where my niece at?" Something about Blaze looked different, but I couldn't put my finger on it.

"I left her ass with her depressing ass mama." Pouring a drink, he sat down next to me.

"What's going on? You done cheated again? Drea if I find out your ass been slipping on dicks again, I'm gone sew that bitch up." When he yelled that shit across the yard, the pastor damn near choked.

"Can you ever be serious? Naw I ain't cheated, but I'm damn sure thinking about that shit. She won't give me no pussy and her ass just different. I ain't sign up for this dumb shit."

"Nigga she did just have a fucking baby."

"Three fucking months ago."

"Yeah you right, me and Drea didn't even wait until her six weeks was up. Man I stuck my dick in and fell all in that pussy. I cried real tears. A nigga thought the baby fucked her shit up."

"You dumb as fuck."

"Nigga I'm dead ass. Shit felt weird as fuck. Told her ass, I can wait. She was horny though so I fucked her with my fist."

"I'm telling you, mama should have got a check for your slow ass."

"You think I'm playing, her shit was wide as hell. One night, I was rocking the baby to sleep right. This mother fucker wanted it so bad, she started grinding against my foot. I kicked her ass dead in the pussy. The nasty bitch moaned." This nigga had me laughing so hard, I was holding my stomach.

"Tell me you playing my nigga."

"Ask her, I swear. Matter fact, don't ask her shit about her pussy. You ain't getting none either, your bitch ass might try to fuck again."

"Fuck you and nigga what the fuck is wrong with your fucking face. I keep trying to figure out what the fuck is different."

"Mind your fucking business." I was staring trying to figure it out, until he flicked his Bic.

"I said change the fucking subject." Laughing, I watched as Paris and Panda walked in. They were in their swim suits and my dick got brick hard. Juicy needed to give me some pussy. A nigga was ready to bend Paris over the grill. Hell or Panda, at this point it really didn't matter.

"Nigga you need some for real. Since you staring at Paris so hard, nut in her edges. I heard that shit grow your hair." Laughing, I swear I hated his ass.

CHAPTER 3- SHADOW

Grabbing our bags from luggage claim, me and Kimmie walked hand in hand. We were hoping that this trip was a success. First my dick wasn't working and now it seems like my damn soldiers ain't marching. I have been trying to get her pregnant since our wedding night and ain't shit shaking but my balls. She don't speak on it, but I can tell it bothers her. All these dick problems was fucking with a nigga mental. I done did a lot of shit in my life, but I don't think a broke dick need to be a nigga's karma. How the hell imma be attracted to hoes, but my dick don't work right. God had a funny since of humor and I ain't laughing.

"You okay baby?"

"Yeah, I'm just thinking this one has to be the one."

"I hope so." Walking to parking, we jumped in my whip and headed out. This girl was everything to a nigga and all she wanted was my seed. If I hadn't wasted all my shit going down a bitch's throat, I may have had some working nut to give her. Every

23

time I see the disappointment on her face, I be wanting to go grab

an ex hoe and snatch my shit out they stomach like here, try these.

If all they ass wasn't dead, I would try anything at this point.

Stopping at home, we wanted to freshen up and shit before we

headed to the cook out. As close as we are, everybody been doing

the family thing and we hadn't been around each other too much

lately. We have managers working the club and business is still

booming. Overall, we were living the good life. Even though I

married the perfect woman, it seems like I'm the only nigga that

didn't get their happy ending. All they ass had kids or their girl

was pregnant. That's why a nigga planned this trip, a change of

scenery might make my eggs move different. It was the perfect trip

even though a mother fucker tried to fuck my shit up.

Sitting on the white sandy beaches in Puerto Rico, I fed

Kimmie strawberries as we drunk champagne. A nigga was trying

to set the mood and I wanted to be lit. It's a many of mother

fuckers who got a bitch pregnant when they were drunk. I know I

should be able to pop my wife off. I was drinking this soft shit now,

but when we got ready to fuck she was getting that Henny dick.

"*Baby, I wish we could live here forever. It's so fucking beautiful.*"

"*It is, but a nigga need them Chicago streets. I done already retired and now you want a nigga living like a lame ass mother fucker eating beans all day.*"

"*I'm gone need you to broaden yourself. Puerto Ricans don't eat beans all day retard.*"

"*Bottom line, the shit ain't happening. I'll bring your ass whenever you want to come, but that's it. Issa hood rat.*"

"*Fuck you, I'm not a damn hood rat.*" *She hit me in the arm as she laughed.*

"*I'm talking about my ass. You think you too good for them streets, but I see your ass got left off bad and boujie.*" *As we laughed, a man walked our way. I thought he would keep going until he stopped.*

"*My boss would like for you to have a word with him at his compound.*"

"*Compound deez nuts. Don't you see me with my girl?*"

"*It's to discuss a very important matter.*"

"Nigga ain't shit more important than my wife and I don't know you niggas. Here take these beans and get the fuck out my face."

"Baby, I told you they don't eat beans like that."

"I forgot, the nigga pissed me off."

"You have to learn to control your anger. There are different ways to handle things."

"Didn't I just tell you I'm a hood rat."

"Excuse me sir." Realizing this nigga was still standing there, I looked over at Kimmie and took a deep breath.

"Sir, can you please tell your boss I respectfully decline. I'm on vacation with my wife and you have about ten seconds to get the fuck out of my face before I slap your ass to sleep. You ever fell asleep on the sand? I could only imagine that shit gets hot in the morning." Turning back to Kimmie, it felt good to see her smiling at me.

"I'm so proud of you. That's a step. Now all you have to do is leave off the threats." When I saw this nigga still standing here, I wondered if his ass was a mute like the nigga Quick killed.

Jumping up to my feet, he took off running when he realized I was

serious.

"Let's go before I fuck around and go to jail out here. I'm

too pretty for that shit. My ass will be fighting all night trying not

to become somebody's burrito."

"Yeah, let's go so I can get your ass a map."

Once we got inside the hotel, we fucked all night. We

didn't leave out the room until it was time to go back home. I

didn't see the nigga again, but curiosity did have me wondering

who the fuck his boss was and how the fuck he knew me. Shit was

strange as fuck if you ask me.

After getting dressed we headed over to Blaze's crib. As

soon as we walked in the yard, the shit felt good. I was so happy to

see my brothers I damn near knocked Kimmie over trying to get

over there to them.

"What up fam."

"Bro I thought you wasn't gone make it. Did you go see a

doctor about your weak ass sperm?"

"Nigga damn, do you joke about everything?" Blaze shrugged his shoulders and kept flipping the meat.

"Don't get mad at me because you walking around with kiddie sperm."

"Fuck you." Leaving that nigga laughing at my expense, I headed over to Baby Face.

"I don't even know why I be excited to see that nigga. He don't even make it a minute before I be ready to knock his ass out."

"Stop fronting bro. You know damn well your ass ain't gone do shit. That nigga itching to set something on fire. Go speak to your mama and her new man." Looking over, I saw her sitting on the pastor lap that married us.

"You know what's fucked up, that nigga did our wedding and I don't even know his name."

"Me either. Fuck him." Laughing at Face, I went to go say hi.

"Hey beautiful." I nodded at the pastor as I bent down to kiss my mama.

"Nigga I don't know where your lips been. Get the fuck on."

"Ma, that's how you talk around the pastor?"

"Nigga please, I cursed his ass out at church Sunday. He was all in this lady face passing her notes and shit. Almost got that hoe a spot on the sick and shut in list."

"Debra, I told you she is the secretary. All I was doing was giving her the church announcements."

"You was about to be announcing her funeral. Fuck you mean."

"Ma, they got a special place in Hell for you. I'm gone pray for you."

"You better pray for Devon. He the one gone need it."

"Who is Devon."

"The pastor. Nigga you about dumb as hell. How you gone let somebody marry you and don't know they name. How you know you and Kimmie really married? Matter fact, don't answer that. Get your slow ass out my face. Who the fuck raised you niggas." She actually got up and walked away as she shook her head. Any nigga that dealt with her had my respect. That mother fucking lady was bat shit crazy. Blaze and Kimmie was arguing as usual and I grabbed her away and took her to sit down. I don't know why she insisted on playing with this nigga. Especially around fire. If I told her ass what he did to Shirree maybe she would leave his ass alone.

"Baby why you pull me away."

"Shut the fuck up, I just saved your life."

"I'm sick of yall." She got up and walked over to Paris and Panda. She can keep playing, but I swear she on her own. Leaning back in my chair, I just smiled. Our lives was great and it felt good as fuck to be around my family.

CHAPTER 4- QUICK

"Where the fuck you coming from ma?" Ash ass been leaving a lot lately and the only reason I didn't think she was cheating is because she had Zavi with her all the time. A nigga didn't want to turn his son into a snitch, so this mother fucker was gone tell me what's up.

"We just ran to the mall."

"When I took you back what did I tell you?"

"What are you talking about Quick?"

"I asked you to never keep anything from me, but that's what you doing right now. You disappearing and shit every damn day. Now you standing in my face lying. Don't make me fuck you up Ashanti, now where the fuck you been?"

"I'm not keeping anything from you baby, please just let me handle it." She got me fucked up and she was really trying me. Grabbing her by her neck, I was ready to choke a booga out her ass.

"What the fuck you mean you gone handle it? I'm your fucking husband and I'm asking you what the fuck is going on." Letting her neck go, I walked away from her before I hurt her ass. She was eight months pregnant and I was trying not to lay hands on her, but she was making the shit hard. "If you don't trust me enough to understand or handle what the fuck is going on, then imma leave and give us some space."

"Baby please. Don't leave, I'm sorry." Sitting down on the couch, she dropped her head in her hands. "I don't think you will understand and I don't want you going off."

"It don't matter how you think I will react. I'm your husband and I ain't doing that sneaky shit. Now what the fuck is going on?"

"Jason been wanting to see Zavi. That's it, he misses him and I didn't think you would get it." When she realized my eyes turned from hazel to smoke gray, she knew she had fucked up. "Quick, he doesn't understand." Walking to the closet, I opened my safe and grabbed my gun. Pointing at her, I let her know where she had me fucked up at.

"Help me understand how you thought I would be okay with you taking my son to see that bitch ass nigga?" Her standing up walking up to me threw me off guard.

"Make this your last time pulling a gun on me and don't use it. You're pissed, I get that. But you better figure out how to use your fucking words before you lose your life. I'm not going through this shit again for nobody. If you feel the only way to get your point across is to put your hands on me, then you can leave."

"Bitch first of all, this my shit. Secondly, don't think I want light your ass up over my child. Thirdly, I see this nigga done gave you some fucking balls. I ain't never disrespected you, yet you keep thinking it's ok to play me like a bitch ass nigga. All I have been is a hunnid with you, but you stay keeping secrets. You can have that shit Ash." Putting my gun away, I walked in the kitchen to pour me a shot of Julio.

"I'm not trying to keep secrets from you, but he is a child. All he knew was Jason and he misses him. I didn't see nothing wrong with allowing him to visit him."

"Let me ask you something. When you take Zavi to see him, what does he call him?" When she started looking stupid, I knew the answer.

"Daddy Jason. Look, before you snap off."

"Get the fuck out of my face Ash. Matter fact, give me your phone."

"Why do you want my phone?"

"Because you obviously don't know how to tell a nigga to fuck off and I'm gone help you out before I have to kill you." Reaching in her pocket, she passed it to me and then stormed off. Walking up to Zavi's room, I figured it was time for a talk.

"Hey son, what you doing?"

"Playing the game."

"Turn it off, come talk to me for a second." When he walked over, I pulled him to me. I wanted him to understand what I was about to say, but I didn't want him to think he was in trouble. "I know you grew up with Jason and you miss him, but you hurt daddy's feelings when you go to see him. It hurts even more when you call him daddy. Do you want to hurt my feelings lil man?"

"No daddy I don't."

"Then you can't do that anymore okay. I'm your only daddy and when you leave to see him, I miss you."

"Okay, daddy I won't. I only want you. Just don't leave me too okay." That shit hurt my heart and I see that Jason putting them out really fucked my lil man's head up.

"I told you, I'm not going anywhere. Now get ready so we can go see your granny, uncles and cousins."

"Okay daddy, just one more turn okay." Laughing, I stood up to walk out.

"Okay, just one more." When I walked out the room, Ash dumb ass was standing outside the door. I walked pass her like I didn't even see her creep ass. When I got to the room, I jumped in the shower so I can start getting ready. Just as I was starting to wash up, she got in with me.

"I know you are mad at me, but I wasn't trying to keep anything from you. You get so upset and I'm afraid to tell you some things."

"Look, I know I got a temper. That still don't give you the right to keep something like that from me. I'm your fucking husband and if I can't trust you, the shit won't work Ash. Do better my nigga or you gone lose me."

"Why do you always do that? Every time shit don't go your way, you threaten to leave. That shit ain't cool and it makes me feel like you want me walking on egg shells."

"With the dumb shit you be pulling, you need to tip toe on them mother fuckers. You like to play victim, but you be doing some foul shit. We have to go at this shit together or not at all." Rinsing off, I got out of the shower because she wasn't getting this shit. If she didn't think the shit was wrong, she wouldn't have hid it and lied. I'm not about to play these games with her ass.

Once we were done, we headed over to Blaze's house. The ride in the car was quiet except the noise from Zavi's iPad. This mother fucker had the nerve to be sitting over there pouting like somebody stole her fucking bike. When we pulled up to the house, I jumped out of the car fast as hell. A nigga wasn't with all that depressing shit. Even though she was eight months pregnant, I left her ass to waddle on her own. She did the stupid shit, now she need to own it. Walking in the back yard, everybody was laughing and having a good time. A nigga got excited as hell.

"Hoover Gang in the mother fucking building." They all turned and looked at me. My brothers got excited and I decided to get shit cracking. "Hoovers, front and center." They dumb asses walked over to me and didn't have to question what I was on. Throwing our shades on, we stood in front of the family doing the brother line. Our dumb asses stood there waving and shit and even though we weren't at the club, it felt good as hell.

"Sit yall dumb asses down looking like a gay version of the Five Heartbeats." Our mama sholl had a way of crushing a nigga's spirits.

"You been real slick at the mouth now that you done found a new man. Don't forget your old ass was just getting stretched out by our gay ass daddy. Mother fuckers get some human hair and don't know how to act."

"Fuck you Blaze." Mama got up and went in the house with the pastor on her heels.

"Please tell me the pastor is not her new man."

"Yup and his nasty ass going to Hell." Baby Face confirmed that bullshit.

"Mama about to turn his ass out."

"Yall be going in on mama like she ain't supposed to find love."

"Shadow shut yo dumb ass up and help your mama find a cute wig since you wanna do something."

"Nigga what the fuck wrong with your face?" He didn't even respond to me, the nigga just flicked his Bic. His ass wasn't gone ever change.

CHAPTER 5- BLAZE

Hearing the doorbell ring, I walked away from the family and went to open the door. Everybody was here but Juicy, so I assumed it was her. As soon as I opened it, a nigga and his security was standing there.

"The fuck your big ass want? You came to my door strong ass fuck my nigga. I'll sell your ass a plate this time, but I ain't with that friendly neighbor shit. And yo big ass gone get some string beans. You look like the type that want all the meat and shit."

"I've been trying to set up a meeting with you and your brothers. Since you won't accept any of my messages, I came personally to talk to you."

"It would have been easier for you to ask for extra meat. We don't know you and therefore you don't have business with us. Now do you want this plate or not fam?"

"You talk a lot of shit for a nigga with only one trick."

Before he could even blink, I had my lighter up to his eye ready to

39

deep fry that mother fucker. His men raised their guns at me and I guess they thought I was worried.

"Even if they shoot me my nigga you won't use this mother fucker no more." Looking over to one of his men, I asked a question. "You ever seen a fat ass pirate?"

"That one trick gone get you dead real quick."

"Try your luck bitch." Turning around, my brothers were behind me with guns drawn. Quick passed me my strap and I pointed it at the fat ass nigga.

"Now what was you saying?" Motioning for his men to drop their weapons, he turned back to us.

"I only came here to talk. Your father owed my boss ten million dollars. I'm here to collect on that debt."

"How the fuck you thought that shit?" Baby Face stepped up and I knew he was ready to end this shit.

"The moment you killed him, that became your debt."

"You got us fucked up. Look, do you still want this plate. Because I ain't got time for this dumb shit."

"If you don't have the money, you can work off your debt. Just know, the debt will be paid. Voluntarily or involuntarily. We would prefer you guys to work for us. You each possess a skill that is useful to our organization. We will give you a week to think about it. Someone will come by here and get your answer. It is in your best interest to accept our offer."

"You got ten seconds to make your exit." Him and Baby Face had a stare down.

"One week." The fat mother fucker walked off and I turned to my brothers.

"Why the fuck didn't we just handle that shit right now? We gone give this nigga time to come back?"

"Because he is not the boss. If we kill him, it still doesn't solve our problem. We need to figure out who the fuck this nigga owed. We have to know what we are up against before we make a decision." Looking at Baby Face, I snapped.

"What you mean a decision? The answer is fuck no. Blaze don't work for no mother fucker and if we give they ass ten million, we have to get back in the business."

"I know all of that. Which is why we need to figure out who it is. If we are going to war, we need to know who we are up against. In the meantime, we need to be careful. These mother fuckers know where we live and can pop up at any time."

"When I was in Puerto Rico a mother fucker came up to us on the beach telling me his boss wanted a meeting with me. I know the vicinity, but I still don't know who it is." Easing my lighter up to Shadow's lip, I flicked that mother fucker.

"What the fuck Blaze. Now ain't the time to be playing."

"Nigga I ain't playing, you stood your dumb ass in my yard for about an hour and ain't told us shit. You sat your ass back there and didn't say a word. I should leave your ass on the porch."

"Leave this dick in your mouth clown ass."

"First off, you gay. Second, nigga your dick never work get your flaccid ass on. Nigga shit can't even say hi, let alone stand up and he talking shit."

"ENOUGH. Damn, can you niggas ever be serious. Everything always a joke to yall. We retired and walked away from this shit and a nigga on your door step threatening to take away everything we worked for and you niggas out here joking."

This nigga Baby Face was pissed.

"Nigga you just need some pussy. Shut the fuck up. You

ready to shoot anything since you can't shoot your shit in your

girl." Shaking his head, Baby Face walked back in the house.

"I should have let them shoot your ass. You aggy as fuck."

Shrugging my shoulders, we headed towards the kitchen. Hearing

moaning, I got pissed.

"Drea, I know your bitch ass ain't slipped on another

dick?" Kicking the door in, me and my brothers stood there in

disbelief as the pastor hit our mama from the back. When Baby

Face snatched our mama up, I grabbed the pastor by his dick and

you already know what happened next. I flicked my mother

fucking Bic. They nasty asses had me fucked up.

"Oh my God. Please stop." He wanted to scream and call

on God now.

"Blaze let him go, I need that dick. I don't want no scabby

penis in my pussy."

"Get the fuck on before that wolf pussy be howling pussy."
Turning away from her, I looked back at the pastor.

"It's kids in my fucking house, don't you ever disrespect
my shit. I will cook your shit and serve it to the fucking masses.
Issa flame broil. Now get your fraud ass out my fucking shit."
Taking the lighter off, he fixed his clothes and ran out the
bathroom.

"Come on Debra, I think we should go." He caught on
quick.

"Nigga you better put some butter on that shit. I'm hungry
as fuck and I want to see my grandbabies. He just helped you feel
what Hell is like. Now you got something to preach about Sunday.
That's some juicy ass shit, I might even stay woke. Come on hot
dick, let me get the butter."

"Your mama just gone make that man sit back there with a
bubbling dick. Something is wrong with all yall." Laughing at
Shadow, we headed outside to finish the party. I couldn't get no
pussy, his ass couldn't either. As soon as we stepped outside,
Kimmie was flipping the meat on the grill.

"Gone girl, we don't want no white people BBQ."

"You always talking shit. I'm not scared of your ass."

Everybody got quiet. We were family and we all talked shit, but I see Kimmie thought it was sweet. She the only one out here who ain't really felt this mother fucker. Grabbing my Bic, she slapped it out of my hand. "What you gone do now brother? You ain't shit without your lighter." Everybody started laughing, until I reached in my pocket and grabbed another one. She turned to Shadow looking for help.

"Run bae, run."

"Nigga you gone let him get your girl?" Quick was laughing at Shadow's scary ass.

"I told her I wouldn't have her back. Girl why the fuck you still standing there, run." Realizing that her husband wasn't coming to her rescue, she looked at me and took off running. Going after her, I was shocked. She was hauling ass. Literally. This big girl was gone, jumping over chairs and all. A nigga was keeping up with her and almost got her until we got to the last chair. My mama dirty ass stuck her foot out and down went

Frazier. I went flying in the pool and I couldn't do shit to stop it. When I came out the water, I leaned on the edge and let my mama know it was on.

"You know I'm gone get your ass back right?"

"Nigga, your eyebrows crying." Looking over at Baby Face, I didn't realize what he meant right away. Then it hit me. Drea's ass watched a you tube video and drew me some eyebrows on since I burnt mine off. The shit must be coming off in the water. They were laughing so hard, I couldn't even get pissed. Climbing out the pool, I shot Drea's ass a look.

"All this fucking money we got and my wife using cheap ass make up."

"Nigga where the fuck are your eyebrows?" Quick was laughing so hard he was crying tears.

"Fuck yall, I made a mistake and burnt them off."

"How you burn your own shit? Nigga them mother fuckers done made a M on your face." I threw my middle finger up at Shadow.

"Da Da cry?" When Spark said that shit, the whole damn yard was crying tears they were laughing so hard. I damn near threw her lil ass in the pool. They got me fucked up.

"Drea bring your ass in the house and come fix my eyebrows. Kimmie this ain't over."

"Fuck with me if you want to, all I gotta do is lick my thumb." Now she had the upper hand on me. I can't wait to my shit grow back. Laughing as I went in the house, I couldn't do shit but wonder was this coming to an end. My family made it out of all that bullshit, only to be dragged back in. A nigga couldn't go to war with fake eye brows what if it got hot? Laughing at myself, I sat down while Drea hooked me up.

"We going to MAC tomorrow. Yall got me fucked up."

CHAPTER 6- BABY FACE

Leaving Blaze house, a nigga was feeling good. My savage was about to be released and I couldn't be happier. Mother fuckers would never understand how much I missed that shit and I would never admit it. I was the one that wanted to walk away from it all, but I didn't know it would have me feeling incomplete. Maybe if I wasn't going through so much shit with Juicy, a nigga could feel good about leaving the life. But sitting at home arguing all damn day wasn't the life I had pictured. Dragging my ass home, it took everything in me to get out my truck and walk in that mother fucker. As soon as I entered the house, I knew something was off. Running upstairs, Juicy and the baby was gone. After the visit we got today, I started to panic and feel like shit for leaving her the way that I did. In my defense, I didn't know we had enemies out here. Grabbing my phone to call my brothers, I glanced up at the closet and saw that it was empty. There is no way a mother fucker took her and let her grab clothes. This bitch left. Running my hands down my face, I walked down the stairs and jumped in my car. How the fuck she walking out and she the mother fucking

problem. Knowing I did some shit in my past that put a strain on

our shit, but a nigga been making up for that shit ever since. Juicy

couldn't be nowhere but at her momma crib. I don't got time for

the stupid shit. Taking the ride across town, I pulled up and her

mama was sitting on the porch holding Zaria.

"Hey ma, what's your daughter's problem now?"

"Honestly, I don't know. She came by here and dropped off

the baby. Said she was leaving and how she need a break. Gave me

all the baby's stuff and was gone. I tried to convince her not to

leave the baby, but something in her eyes wasn't right. Her ass

didn't even look back and she took off." Sitting down next to her

mama, I felt defeated.

"I've tried everything to make that girl happy, nothing

works. How the fuck could she leave our baby like that?"

"I don't know. She is fine here, I know that you're her

father and I'm not taking that from you. Zaria needs a lot of

attention and I know that as much as you would like to give it to

her, you can't. Not all day. She will be here whenever you want her and that way if Juicy stop by she can see her too." Not feeling right about leaving my baby, I thought about what she was saying and with the war that's coming maybe it's for the best.

"Okay ma. I'm going to take her tonight and I'll bring her back tomorrow. You can keep all the stuff you have and I'll get her all new stuff. That way I don't have to keep dragging the stuff back and forth."

"It's going to be okay son. She just needs time."

"To be honest, I don't know if I have it in me to wait. She been treating me like shit for months and I continue to kiss her ass. It ain't in a nigga ma. I have given that girl all of me and it's still not enough. I'll be by here tomorrow." Grabbing Zaria, I strapped her in and drove off. She had me fucked up if she thought she could keep putting our shit on hold whenever she felt like it. I loved Juicy with everything in me, but I'm still me. Grabbing my phone, I called my mama to see what kind of store I needed to go to.

"What you want boy? Yall showed the fuck out today. Now yall got my ass over here sucking burnt dick. The fuck I'm gone do with that hard ass crispy shit? I like my shit medium well you

niggas done gave me Cajun."

"First off ma, I don't wanna here that shit. Second, that was

your favorite child Blaze that did that shit. I was gone shoot his

ass, but I let him be great once Blaze got hold of his ass."

"You could have stopped his ass."

"Ma, you forgot what that nigga did to me. How the fuck

was I gone stop him? I see your ass didn't help either."

"Fuck no I didn't. That wig just look like good hair, but the

shit was synthetic. A spark would have had my ass looking like a

blow torch."

"Ma, I didn't call you to talk about this. Where can I get

some milk from for the baby?"

"Where the slow ass mama at? How the fuck she don't

know that? What the hell yall been feeding that baby?"

"She left and call herself not coming back. The baby with

me now and I need to know where to go."

"Go to Walmart. They will have everything you need.

Clothes and all."

"You fucking tried it. I'm going to the mall tomorrow. You won't have my baby out here looking like buy one get one free."

"Whatever nigga. Jerk chicken over here trying to get some. Call me if you need me." Hanging up, I shook my head in disgust. That lady ought to be ashamed of her damn self.

Pulling in to Walmart, I got Zaria out and walked in the store. As soon as we walked in the door, she started crying.

"Come on baby, don't start that shit right now." She ignored my pleas and kept screaming to the top of her lungs. Rushing to the baby aisle, I was looking at the milk and the shit was giving me a headache. They had powder, liquid, and different brands. The confusion of what I was supposed to get and the baby screaming, I was ready to say fuck this shit and take her to McDonalds.

"You need some help?" Turning around, I noticed the girl didn't work there I guess she was tired of Zaria screaming.

"Please, I'm lost as hell." She reached for Zaria and I side eyed the shit out of her ass.

"Just trust me." I let her get her and she started singing. When Zaria calmed down, I wanted to kick my ass for never trying that. When Juicy was pregnant and having complications, I sung to her and she would settle down. Once she realized Zaria was good, she passed her to me. As soon as she got in my arms, she started crying again. For the second time in my life, I began to sing in public.

"When I see your face, it's not a thing that I would change. Cus girl you're amazing just the way you are. And when you smile, the whole world stops and stare for a while. Cus girl you're amazing just the way you are." As I continued to sing Bruno Mars, the girl started grabbing the milk and water I needed. She walked with me to the register so I could continue to sing to my baby girl. Reaching in my pocket, I paid for my stuff and walked out the door. When I put her in the seat, the lady passed me the bag. Finally getting a chance to look at her, she was a different kind of beautiful. She looked exotic, but had this innocent look about her. Tsunami was ready to attack.

"You're a life saver. What's your name?"

"Royalty."

"That's your real name?" She laughed at my question, I'm guessing she hears that a lot.

"Yeah it is. Are you going to tell me your name?"

"Baby Face and no it's not."

"Your baby is gorgeous. Her mother didn't tell you what you needed to get at the store."

"Her mother is no longer with us."

"Oh my God, I'm sorry for your loss."

"She ain't dead. Yet." I mumbled the last part.

"This may be bold of me, but take my number just in case you need me." Handing her my phone, I let her put it in and she called her number. Saying our goodbyes, I headed out.

"I'll call you soon." Getting in my truck, I started to feel guilty. Fuck that, she left me. I'm a fucking Hoover, you don't put us on hold when you feel like it. Bitch had me fucked up. I'm that nigga. She was gone learn that shit quick.

CHAPTER 7- SHADOW

"Bae, what is wrong with your brother? That fool done burnt his own shit off. He is so fucking funny. He thought he had my ass."

"You don't even know what you started. That nigga not gone stop until he gets the last laugh."

"He ain't gone do shit, his ass don't want these problems."

"I'm just letting you know, when he gets your ass back it's gone be fucked up. You ever wondered what the hell happened to Mack?" Looking at me crazy, she got quiet.

"No, I didn't want to know."

"All you need to know is he put that nigga lip in Baby Face mouth and they still wasn't even. He don't like for people to have an advantage over him. I promise he won't quit until he gets the last laugh. You better sleep with your eye open."

"Eye? Nigga you acting like I ain't got two."

"Baby you know damn well one of them mother fuckers is sleepy. You be talking and your shit dead ass take a nap."

"Fuck you and your brothers." Grabbing her around her waist, I picked her up.

"You know you just want to fuck daddy."

"All I know is your ass better not drop me." Putting her down, I laughed.

"You right. Mother fuckers be talking about issa snack. Your ass a whole meal." She tried to hit me and I ran up the stairs. As soon as we got to the room, I slammed her on the bed.

"You know I love you right? No matter what happens as far as the baby goes, it won't change how I feel about you."

"Thank you, but I want to be a mother. I want to give you your first child."

"If I can help it, you will. But you have to quit swallowing though. You can't get pregnant that way."

"Get your dumb ass off me. All you mother fuckers ignorant. Starting with your mama."

"I'm telling on your ass." Kissing her, I slid my tongue in her mouth and just like that play time was over. Sitting up, I grabbed her by her ankles and slid her to the floor.

"Damn nigga, you done hurt my whole damn back."

"That bitch got some cushion. Now shut the fuck up, I'm trying to get in them guts." Pulling her pants off, I got her panties off and threw to the side. Her body was perfect and I loved every last curve. Leaning her legs back over her head, I laid on top of them and started doing sit ups in her pussy. I needed my nut to go straight to the egg.

"Damn baby. I don't think I can take this position."

"You gone take this dick and you gone love it." Going faster, I made sure my dick was reaching the bottom. When I felt her body shaking, I jumped up and put my mouth over her pussy.

"Cum in daddy mouth." And just like that, she did. Catching all her juices, I sat up and slid my dick back in while her body was still going through it.

"Cum on daddy dick." When she started grinding back, I knew my nut was about to make an appearance soon.

"Cum with me daddy."

"Fuck girl, I'm cumming." Spreading her legs as far as I could, I started slamming my dick hard as hell in that pussy. My curve caused me to lay on her spot.

"FUUUUCCCKKKK." Rubbing her clit, her body started shaking as I came all in that pussy. Rolling over on my side, I prayed this was our baby. She got up and went to get in the shower, I looked at all that ass shaking and I can't believe this was my first BBW. She was so fucking sexy to me. Trying to gather my thoughts so I could get in the shower with her, I heard her scream.

"Nigga you gave me carpet burn, I should beat your ass."

"Girl it only took off one layer, you got plenty more quit crying." I could hear her talking shit and I decided to wait to shower by my damn self. She gets petty when she mad and I'm too tired for that shit. When she walked out, I got my ass in and I couldn't wait to get my ass in the bed. We been fucking none stop trying to get her pregnant. We fucked in Puerto Rico before we jumped on the plane and went straight to Blaze house. A nigga was tired. I was just happy my shit was working. My ass didn't ever want to go through that shit again. Not even bothering to put on clothes, I laid in the bed. Kimmie was already sleep before my head hit the pillow. Shortly after, my ass was knocked out.

Hearing a mother fucker laughing, I jumped out of my sleep. This nigga blaze was standing over Kimmie in the dark. Cutting the light on, I could only imagine what the fuck he was up to. This nigga had a pamper, spreading baby shit all over Kimmie.

"Nigga what the fuck are you doing?"

"She thought she was hot shit earlier when she knocked my lighter out my hand, now she about to literally be hot shit." Before I could stop him, this nigga flicked his Bic and the shit caught flame. It was the worse smell ever.

"Kimmie get the fuck up. GET UP BEFORE THAT SHIT START MELTING IN MY BED." She jumped up out of her sleep and saw the flame. "How the fuck you didn't feel that shit?" She ran her big ass to the shower so fast, the baby shit was flying off her arm. "Man, your ass getting these shit chunks up before you lay your ass back down." I hated this nigga Blaze. I swear his ass play all his fucking life. Who thinks of nasty ass shit like this.

59

"Hey nigga, I know why you can't get your girl pregnant."

"Don't start that shit."

"Nigga your damn dick broke. That mother fucker pointing too far left. The nut hitting her walls. How the fuck is it gone go up if the mother fucker blind. Nigga just out here all wrong running into walls and shit. Fix that shit. Don't nobody want no hanger in they pussy."

"Get the fuck out of my house bro."

"Gladly, yall need to clean up in here. Your girl nasty as fuck. It smells like straight shit in this mother fucker and your ass just in her sleep."

"BLAZE GET OUT."

"Aight nigga. It's a couple of chunks by her pillow though. You might wanna get that just in case she sleeps with her mouth open. Then again, maybe you don't care. You like bitches that eat shit and suck booty holes. Nigga seriously though, it's a booty hole." When he saw me rub my hand down my face, he threw his hands up and walked out. Opening a window, I tried to get the smell out. That shit wasn't working and I wondered what the fuck

Spark had ate for lunch. Her ass smell like a grown ass nigga. Kimmie walked out the bathroom and you could see the steam coming from her ass she was so mad.

"Don't look at me like that. I told your ass."

"That nigga need to be admitted. He only do this shit because yall let him."

"You're more than welcome to try and stop him. Oh and he said you got shit on your pillow. I'm going to the guest room, I can't sleep in here."

"You not gone help me?'

"Hell naw. I told you don't start a war with him. You ain't ready for his kind of petty."

"Fuck your scary ass then."

"Good night shitty." Laughing I went and laid my ass down to get some sleep.

CHAPTER 8- QUICK

"You really not gone give me my phone back? I told you that I wouldn't keep shit else from you."

"Ash, you told me that when I took your ass back and here we are again. You can quit asking, I'm not giving it back just yet."

"You not slick, you just waiting to see if Jason gone message me."

"Well duh dummy. It took you that long to figure the shit out? You know I ain't letting that shit fly. This nigga on his way."

"On his way where?"

"The upper room." When I sung the shit like Eddie Murphey, she sucked her lips and got mad. "You sucking them lips, come suck on something else." Her eyes lit up like she thought it could get her phone back. She can think I'm playing if she wants to, but as soon as I find out where this nigga at, he dead as Paris's edges. Leaning down, she pulled my dick out and started caressing it. Shit felt good as fuck and I couldn't wait for her to get this big mother fucker in her mouth. As if she could hear my thoughts, she deep throated my shit. Her ass wasn't even playing around with this mother fucker. Before she started getting a good stroke going, her text message beeped and I damn near broke her neck trying to get up to get the phone.

"I'm sorry baby."

"Damn nigga. Be careful. How the fuck I'm gone tell the doctor I got whiplash from dick?"

"I'll just pull this mother fucker out and they will understand."

"Shut up." Looking down at the phone, I got happy as hell when I saw it was that nigga.

J: Can I see my son today?

Me: Yea, where you want to meet?

J: come by the house about 9.

Me: Ok.

Looking over at Ash ass, I got pissed all over again.

"Why the fuck this nigga want you to come so late?"

"I don't know. Ask him."

"It don't matter. You won't be meeting his ass no more. You better pray your ass ain't fucked him."

"Quick, don't play with me like that. I would never cheat on you. This shit is getting out of hand all because he wanted to see Zavi."

"You should have told the nigga no, now the nigga can go visit all the kids of mine that didn't make it when you swallowed they ass. He not living to see tomorrow I'm about to go handle this shit right now." Throwing my Air Max 95's on, I headed out the door. Sending a message to my brothers, I told them to meet at the main house.

We all damn near pulled up together and I got out and unlocked the door. Stepping inside, I cut the lights on and waited for them to come in.

"What's up Quick?" You can tell Shadow ass was ready to get back to his girl. He was the only one who didn't miss the life. All he thinks about is what if he didn't make it back to Kimmie.

"Ash been going to see that nigga Jason."

"Damn bro, your girl got slip and slide pussy too?" This nigga Blaze was actually looking like we had something in common.

"I don't know my nigga. She said he wanted to see Zavi. Her ass been taking my son to see this clown ass nigga."

"You want to kill him for visiting with your son?" This mother fucker Baby Face acting like we ain't killed for less.

"I'm with you bro. You see Mack ass had to go. Only nigga fucking my bitch and live to tell about it is me."

"And Baby Face." That nigga turned around and looked at Shadow so fast when he said his name. They were determined to get his ass fucked up. Nigga hair just grew back in and they kicking it back off. When Blaze flicked his Bic, I got back on the subject.

"Look, that nigga don't have claims to my son. He playing on Ash because he wants her back. Nigga told her to meet him tonight. Who wants to play with a kid this late? Not me, only kids I'm playing with at that time is the nut I'm shooting down her throat. Them bitches be playing hop scotch."

"She ain't fucking that nigga. Her ass eight months pregnant." I agreed with Baby Face, but still.

"Nigga Drea was eight months." Me and Baby Face turned and looked at Shadow at the same time. This nigga was on good bullshit. Blaze walked up to Shadow and rubbed his lighter across his lip.

"It's all good yall. He just pissed because I rubbed Spark's shit on his girl and set that shit on fire. Now they can be mad together. That's the lighter that had the shit on it." Shadow took off running and we fell out laughing.

"Nigga you need a check."

"When you trying to do this? I gotta go get the baby."

"Now nigga." I looked at Baby Face like he was crazy. We never let a nigga make it. When Shadow walked back in the room, we strapped up and headed out. It wasn't nine, but I wanted to catch the nigga off guard. Parking down the street, we crept up the block and tried the door.

"Mother fuckers gone get enough of leaving their doors unlocked." We crept in and headed upstairs. He had to be up there because all the lights were off. Easing the bedroom doors open, we kept trying until we found the right one. He was laid in between a bitch pussy wearing her shit out.

"Nigga you keep eating the pussy like that, her shit gone be WOE." Not giving him the chance to get up, I shot his ass up. Nigga head didn't even get out the pussy. When the chick started screaming, I shut her up quick. My ass done got rusty, I hit her in the eye and I was aiming for her forehead.

"Damn nigga. You ain't give us a chance to do shit. We didn't get to have fun with they ass."

"Nigga all you wanted to do was burn they ass. Just set the house on fire and let's go." We let Blaze do his thing and got the fuck up out of there. I dropped them niggas off and rushed my ass back home. She was about to finish sucking this dick.

When I walked in the door, this retarded mother fucker was sitting on the couch holding Zavi and they were crying. My dick went soft and my pimp hand got hard. She was really trying me and pushing me to my limit.

"Son, go get ready for bed. I'll be up in a minute to make sure you good." Waiting until he walked off, I turned to Ash and snapped. "I really pray that it's the baby that got you losing your mother fucking mind."

"Baby, I don't give a fuck about Jason, but he was a part of my life for years. He was the only father your son knew up until recently. We have a right to grieve him."

"You about to have the right to get put to sleep. He was the only father Zavi knew because of your bullshit. You decided to keep my son from me. Don't act like I was a dead beat and wouldn't be there."

"Whatever the reason is don't matter. At the end of the day, he was still there."

"And now he not so what you saying?"

"You just don't get it."

"And you pushing me to my fucking limit." Walking off, I headed to Zavi room with a lot on my mind. Shit was crazy.

CHAPTER 9- DEBRA

I know everybody trying to figure out how the hell my ratchet ass end up with a pastor. The day at the wedding, I cursed his ass clean out, but he still wanted me. For some reason that shit turned me on. A man that can want you how you are and don't try to change you is a winner in my book. Leaving the wedding, I still had no intentions to mess with Devon. My kids have their own lives going on and even though I know they love me, they don't come around that often now. They ass didn't even bother to see if I was okay after the shit with Rico. They make decisions for all of us and feel as if you have to deal with it. Don't get me wrong, Rico ass had to go. That nigga was foul as fuck, but he was the only man I had known. I loved that man with every part of me and not once have they asked me how I'm doing. All they ass do is drop my bad ass grand kids off, eat, and go back home. Being the G that I am, my ass played shit off cool, but I was hurting bad. Tired of sitting in the house crying looking like the ugly son at the end of

LOVE AND WAR 4   LATOYA NICOLE

The Color Purple going hey ma ma, I decided to take my ass to bingo. That was when I ran back into Devon.

I hope they ass don't be in here cheating, I will tear this church up over my coins. Taking my seat, I got aggravated when two old bitches came and sat next to me.

"Damn all these seats in here and yall choose to sit by me. You got walkers and shit, take that mess over there. A bitch ain't got room to stamp her damn card."

"You are in a church." The lady had the nerve to look appalled.

"Good, you can die and have your funeral in the same night. Get the fuck out my face." Knowing I wasn't with the shits, she got her old ass up and left. When I glanced over, I realized she called herself telling. Laughing to myself, I set up my cards and chips at my table.

"Miss, we had some complaints." When he realized who I was, he stopped in his tracks. "We meet again Miss Hoover."

"Just call me Debra, you ain't gotta try and be fancy and shit. We too old to be trying to play games."

70

"Okay Debra, it's good to see you again. I see you don't cut people a break even when they in church. Just try to keep it down."

"If yall leave me the fuck alone, I'll be silent. I'm just trying to play my game in peace."

"Okay, gone head I'll talk to you after if you don't mind." I nodded my head so he can leave. *The real reason I wanted they ass gone was so I can pull out my cheat cards. Mother fuckers was trying to fuck up my win. As soon as the caller started doing the numbers, I started racking up. My ass cleaned that church clean out. I got all the money. Ain't nowhere for me to go but hell after this shit, I'll rob the devil of his fire if my ass got cold. Laughing at myself, I tucked my money in my purse. The old ladies eased they ass pass me on their walkers talking shit. When they got to me, I tripped one of them and she almost had a heart attack trying to catch herself from falling.*

"You don't want these problems. Keep it moving Blanch."

"You are something else." Turning around, Devon was standing there and for some reason he looked sexy.

"Been that way all my life. What do you want with me? We live two different worlds and as you can see, my ass ain't gone even be able to look in Heaven's window."

"You never know, people change."

"I'll never change. I'm gone die a shit talking sinner with good pussy. You don't want this in your life. The more you deal with me the further Heaven gone get from your ass."

"Let me judge that for myself." Liking his style, my tiger started purring. My shit was too old to be a cat. Grabbing him by his hand, I walked him out to my car.

"Come talk to me pastor." He got in the car not knowing I was about to snatch his religion. As soon as he sat down, I grabbed his dick and pulled it out. I sucked that man soul in four minutes and he been following my ass around since.

Being with Devon was totally different than being with Rico. He was attentive and no matter what I said or did to him, he tried to make me happy. We went on dates, took walks, and we read to each other. Granted I be reading him shit like *She wanted the streetz, he wanted her heart by A.J Davidson.* And I be sleep while he be reading me the bible, but it's the thought that counts.

His sex is good as hell too. Never thought a pastor could lay it

down like that, but he be taming my ass. Even though I have more

money than him, I never spend a dime of my own shit. The only

thing I hate is he is the pastor. Nigga be wanting me at church

every Sunday and throughout the week. I done told him I'm not fit

to be no damn first lady.

"Baby are you ready?" Looking at him like he was crazy, I

hope he wasn't talking about church.

"For what?"

"I told you I have revival this week. It's a service every

day."

"You have revival. Who in their right mind would sit in

church every damn day Devon? My grandbaby on her way over

here and my ass is tired. You just fucked my booty hole loose and

you want me to go sit in somebody church. What if the Holy Ghost

hit me? Shit juice gone be everywhere."

"You know dang on well the Holy Ghost ain't coming near

you. Just do it for me."

"Not today. I'm tired and we literally just got through fucking. You gone be in church smelling like burnt coochie. This tiger is WOE, I need some rest. Gone now and have a good time. Pray for me baby." He just shook his head and left out. God knew I wasn't shit, he made me. I just hope he remember he did this shit when it was time for me to try and get in them gates. Walking to the tub, I ran me some water. A bitch need to soak after that last session. I'm getting too old for this shit.

CHAPTER 10- BABY FACE

With so much on my mind, I headed over to Juicy's mom house to pick up Zaria. It's crazy how just months ago a nigga was walking down the aisle and vowing his love forever. Now my bitch gone and I have no idea what the fuck her problem was. The shit hurt, but I would never admit it to her ass. It's been three weeks now and she hasn't even called my phone once. Pulling up, I saw her car parked in the driveway and I felt hopeful. Ringing the bell, she answered the door and rolled her eyes as soon as she saw it was me. You would think I did something to her bald headed ass.

"You not gone speak to your husband?"

"Hi." She threw her hand up and walked off.

"Juicy let me talk to you outside for a minute."

"Damn nigga all the fuck you want to do is talk. What." She had an attitude and stomped all the way out the door. It took everything in me not to lay hands on her ass. When I got out the door, I sat down next to her and just looked at the girl I gave my heart to. She was not the same and the shit was baffling me.

"What's wrong baby? Something is obviously bothering you and I want to know what it is. What can I do to fix it, to fix us?"

"You ain't did nothing. I just need some space. Can't a bitch get a break?"

"Parents don't get to take a break. Married couples don't get to take a break Juicy. We figure it out and do what we can to get back on track, but I can't do the shit by myself."

"Get a divorce then Face. I'm tired and if you don't want me to get some rest then leave. I'm not trying to hold you back, as of right now I'm done. You can have it." Even though a nigga would kill niggas for less, she hurt a nigga. Getting up, I walked in the house and got Zaria.

"She'll come around son. Give her time."

"She don't have to. Her ass wants space, she got it. With all due respect, fuck Juicy." Walking out the door, I saw she was still sitting in the same spot just staring into space. She didn't even get up to say bye to our daughter. She finally turned her head and looked me in my eyes. I never broke my stare.

"There's never a right time to say goodbye, but we know that we gotta go our separate ways. And I know it's hard, but I gotta do it and it's killing me it's never a right time a right time to say goodbye." Singing Goodbye by Chris Brown, I let a couple tears fall as she cried. Never moving, she just stared at me with her faces soaked in tears. Turning away, I walked down the stairs and got in my car. I couldn't do this with her. If she wanted out, that's what I was going to give her. Driving home, I felt like less than a man. As soon as we got in the house, Zaria started with her normal routine. The screams were piercing my soul, because I shouldn't be here doing this by myself. My ringing phone brought me out of my trance.

"Hey, is everything ok over there?"

"Yeah it's good." It was Royalty and her voice calmed me.

"It don't sound like it's good over there. What's your address, I'm coming over. That baby gone be sick the way you are letting her scream like that."

"I'm not really in the mood for company."

"That's fine, I'm not coming to see you anyway. Text me your address." She hung up the phone and after thinking it over, I said fuck it. This was what she wanted right. Why the fuck am I over here sad and depressed and shit because my wife chose to leave me and my baby for no fucking reason. Texting her the address, I got up and got my baby girl.

"Daddy will never leave you. I got you Za." Singing to her, I rocked her to sleep and laid her in the play pen. Royalty must have been close by because my bell rung. When I opened the door, I had to tell my dick to sit down. She was in some booty shorts and that ass was sitting nice. With her hair pulled off her face, you could see her features more.

"I brought dinner, have you eaten?"

"Naw, what you got?"

"Tour of Italy's from Olive Garden." Showing her the kitchen, we sat down and ate. It was easy to talk to her and I liked that about her. Before I knew it, I had told her everything about me and Juicy.

"Well just give her some time. You don't know what's going on with her. Just see if she comes around."

"Naw, I'm not that nigga. She wanted out, she got it."

"Good, at least now I don't feel like a home wrecker." Not sure what she meant, I understood clear when she got up and sat on my lap. Once her mouth touched mine, Juicy was the furthest thing from my mind.

"Tell me you want me." What the fuck, that's my line. Her ass was sitting here sounding like a whole nigga right now. My mouth betrayed me and made me a straight bitch.

"I want you."

"Take this shit off." Her aggression was turning me on, but it was scaring me at the same time. I'm the nigga and she was in here treating me like a whole hoe. My ass damn near felt violated, but I got up and took my clothes off. "Mmmm, perfect." She dropped down to her knees and took my entire dick in her mouth. She was sucking my shit so good, my ass felt dizzy. When she stood up and dropped her shorts, I was mesmerized until she tried to sit on my dick.

"Hold on ma, you got a condom?" Being married, I didn't need them mother fuckers no more.

"Naw, but we good." She tried to slide down anyway, grabbing her by her waist, I stopped her.

"We not good ma. I fuck around and fuck you raw today then in four months you got a baby on your back. I'm straight."

"What you mean?"

"It's irrelevant ma. The shit ain't happening without a rubber."

"Fuck it then." This crazy bitch jumped up threw her clothes on and walked out the door. She actually slammed that mother fucker and I sat there speechless until Zaria started screaming. I should catch her and beat her ass. These hoes ain't got no manners. Getting up, I locked my door and grabbed the baby. Heading upstairs, I sung to her until she fell asleep. Jumping in the shower, I handled my business and laid down. My mind drifted back to Royalty. She was crazy as fuck, but that shit just turned me on. Grabbing my phone, I called her and she picked up.

"What's up."

"You don't have to act like that. You shouldn't want to fuck me without a rubber. My ass could have anything, you don't know me."

"Whatever. Look, is that all you wanted? I'm about to go handle some business." This bitch was hell.

"Aight, I'll hit you up tomorrow." Looking at the phone, I realized she had already hung up. Laughing, I closed my eyes. Royalty didn't know who the fuck I was, but she was gone find out soon. I'm gone tame the shit out that ass.

CHAPTER 11- DREA

This was the only thing about being a parent that was hard. These kids will keep your ass on your toes. I was embarrassed as hell when my baby walked in on mommy and daddy being freaky. Blaze nasty ass wanted to keep going. People ask me all the time how the hell I deal with him, but I loved him just as he is.

That nigga gives me so much life and he keeps me laughing. That's how I know we were meant to be. This aggy ass nigga was my soul mate. Strapping Spark down, I jumped in the car and headed to Jewels.

Walking through the grocery store, I thought about how far we had come. Everything was going great in all of our lives. Looking down at Spark, I smiled as she reached for the lighter fluid.

"No baby, we don't play with that." Looking up at me with her bright gray eyes, she smiled. I swear this baby was only a year old and I can tell she was going to be just like her daddy. She was

82

attracted to anything with a flame and I tried my best to keep her away from the shit. Since she was sitting in the buggy, I stepped a couple feet away to get her some grapes. Thinking she needed to eat more fruit, I grabbed some bananas. Turning around, I went to place the items in the cart.

"What the fuck. Spark. Spark baby where are you?" Not wanting to think the worse, I walked around the store praying she climbed out of the buggy. Starting to panic, I stopped anybody walking by.

"Excuse me, have you seen a little girl? She has grey eyes, curly hair, and she has on all pink."

"No I'm sorry." Fuck, Blaze was about to kill me. Running to the front, I had the manager say it over the loud speaker.

"If anybody sees a little girl wearing all pink by herself, please bring her to the front desk."

"Can you give them her description?"

"Ma'am, I'm sure that there is only one baby walking around by their self." Ready to slap his ass, I let him be great and took off running around the store to look for her. The more time that passed, the more tears fell down my face. Reality was starting to set in, my baby was not in this store.

"Can the mother of the missing child please come to the front desk." When I heard that over the loud speaker, I took off running towards the front. Thank God they found her. When I got to the desk, I didn't see her and I didn't understand what the fuck was going on.

"One of our staff members said they saw a man carrying her out of the store and put her into a van. Was it her father? Do you need us to call the police?" Ignoring his questions, I took off running to the parking lot. Her shoe was laying by the curb and I broke down. Grabbing my phone, I made the call I never thought I would have to make.

"Baby, get to Jewels right now."

"What's wrong Drea?"

"Somebody kidnapped Spark."

"If my baby not there by the time I make it, you gone be one dead hoe." Knowing I didn't want to face Blaze's wrath, I went back in the store and prayed the man saw the wrong baby.

84

As soon as Blaze walked in, I knew it was about to be all bad. His face expression showed me he was coming with the bull shit. I didn't expect him to blame me though. When he choked slammed me into the wall, I thought a hoe was gone need CPR. It wasn't his normal bullshit as choke, he was actually trying to take my ass out.

After reviewing the tape, we left out and headed home to get some belongings. Staying at the main house was a good idea, but I wish they had thought of it before these mother fuckers took my baby. Wondering if they were feeding her or if she was crying for us was breaking my heart.

Why the fuck would they take our child. Our baby girl. She is only one year old. Pulling up to the house, I got out crying. Blaze was trying to look like he had it figured out, but you can tell he was going through it. I didn't mean to blame him, but he was putting the shit on me. He knew damn well the person that took her was after the damn Hoover Gang. The shit was surreal looking at her stuff as I walked in her room. Sitting on the floor, I broke down.

"Baby, I'm gone get her back. Have faith in your man. You're right, this is on me and I'm going to fix it. I promise to get her back, even if I have to give my own life."

"Nigga both of yall better come back. I can't make it without you baby. I won't go through that again. That was the worst year of my life."

"Bitch please. You slid on two dicks and I was only gone six months." Hitting him in his arm, I started laughing.

"Your ass can't stay serious for shit. Come on let's pack."

"I'm just saying." He walked out the room and I grabbed some of Spark belongings just in case they got her back and we still had to stay at the main house.

"Baby you seen my lighters? I can't find none of them mother fuckers. You hiding my shit?" As soon as he said it, I was grabbing Spark's shoes and a bunch of Bics fell out.

"This shit don't make no sense."

"That's right. She daddy's baby you can't fight that shit." Shaking my head, I couldn't believe the harder I tried to keep her from fire, she was drawn to it anyway. "Hurry up. We gotta go."

Taking one last look at her room, I left out. Praying. I needed my

baby to come home, but I didn't want Blaze to give his life either. I

needed both of them like I needed air to breathe. They were my life

and all I had was them. I can't believe this shit was happening now

after everything was going perfect. God please protect my baby

and bring both of them home safe.

CHAPTER 12- BLAZE

"Drea draw my shit on right. Don't have me walking in the barbershop with my eyebrows leaking and shit."

"You bought the good kind so it ain't gone do that."

"Aight, cus them niggas will clown me for life and I'll have to burn that bitch to the fucking ground."

"One day your Bic ain't gone work and your ass gone be in trouble."

"I been thinking about how mother fuckers been trying me lately. I hit up my homie and I got some shit coming in. Niggas gone walk in silence when they see that bitch."

"Oh Lord. I thought you retired?"

"From the life baby, I'm Blaze until I die. Well, when I die for real this time." She laughed and it felt like my shit went crooked. "Stop laughing and shit. Man if your ass have me walking around looking like I'm asking niggas Hmm all day, I'm gone fuck you up."

"Shut up, I got this." Pulling her down to my lap, I started kissing her. My bitch was so fucking fine, no chick out here was touching her. Pushing her against my dick, she stopped drawing and leaned down to kiss me. Sliding her shorts to the side, I pulled my dick out and slid it in.

"Girl I can sleep in this pussy. Damn baby." When she started winding her hips, my dick got brick hard. Cuffing her ass, I started bouncing her up and down on my dick.

"That's right girl, ride that dick." Slapping her ass, she went harder on a nigga dick and I knew I was about to nut. Her pussy was so wet and tight, it's like she was pulling my nut out with her walls.

"Horsie. Horsie." This bad ass baby done crept up on our ass.

"Spark, get your ass out of here."

"Me horsie." Dammit, now her ass thinks I'm about to play and shit and I'm trying to get a nut.

"Daddy play with you in a minute. I'm trying to play in mommy's."

"You better not." She slapped me and I turned my body so she could climb off. Sliding my blue ass dick back in my pants, she grabbed Spark cock blocking ass. Now all of a sudden, her ass ain't thinking about no damn horse and my dick about to bust and shit. When I saw Drea bent over playing with Spark, I walked up behind her and started grinding my dick against her big ass.

"Baby, stop I got your child."

"And I got some kids you can swallow. Don't leave me like this please."

"I got you later on. We about to go to the store so I can cook. You can hold off until tonight." Pissed, I walked off on her ass. Soon as she leaves the house, Jen the deep throater was getting this nut. My ass was gone watch some porn and nut all on her MacBook.

When her and Spark left, I headed upstairs when the doorbell rang. Fuck. Putting my dick up, I ran down and opened the door. Two big greasy ass men was on my porch.

"Our boss wants to know if you have an answer."

"The answer is get your big ass off my damn porch."

"I'll take that as a no."

"Take it as a you gone be getting my porch fixed if that mother fucker cracked when you move." He smirked at me and walked off.

"Sleep light Mr. Blaze."

"Nigga eat light. The fuck." Slamming the door, I came to terms that this nut was gone have to be put on hold and I hit my brothers up. Whoever this clown was, he getting real friendly just showing up at my shit. After I told Baby Face to hit his boy up and find out where these mother fuckers lay their head, I went upstairs to get dressed. Too pissed to jerk my dick off, I decided to gone and head to the barber shop. Heading out, I jumped in the Maybach and drove off. I hadn't even made it to the city when my phone rung. Seeing it was Drea, I started to let that mother fucker go to voicemail since she wants to play with a nigga's nut.

"What girl?"

"Baby, get to Jewels right now."

"What's wrong Drea?"

"Somebody kidnapped Spark." This mother fucker done let somebody take my baby. It's a nigga out here that don't value their life.

"If my baby not there by the time I make it, you gone be one dead hoe." Ending the call, I dialed Baby Face.

"Nigga, tell everybody to meet me at the Jewels down the street from my house. Somebody kidnapped Spark. We need an address on these mother fuckers like yesterday.

"I'm on it. We gone get her back bro." Hanging up, all kinds of shit went through my mind. When I pulled into the Jewels, I had murder on my mind. As soon as I walked up on Drea, I grabbed her ass around her neck.

"How the fuck did they get my baby? Where the fuck was you?"

"I turned away to get her some bananas. She was in the cart. Baby I'm sorry, I don't know what happened." Letting her go, I tried to calm down so I could get the story.

"Then how the fuck do you know she was kidnapped?"

"Because the guy that work here said someone told him a man walked out of here with her. When I went outside, her shoe was on the ground." Punching my hand through the wall behind her, it took everything in me not to fuck her up.

"You carried her ass for nine months with a loose ass pussy and didn't lose her one time. How the fuck did you lose her in a fucking grocery store?"

"Her being kidnapped is because of your lifestyle, not mine. Don't try and turn this shit around on me." Choke slamming her ass against the wall, I was about to fuck her up. Not because she was talking shit, but I knew she was right. This shit was all my fault and knowing what was going on, I shouldn't have let them out of my sight.

"Bro, let her go. This ain't the place." With tears in my eyes, I turned to Baby Face and I let her down. I knew I was losing it, but this was my seed. My baby girl. She ain't have nothing to do with this shit. Walking toward customer service, I approached the man at the counter.

"Let me see your surveillance tapes."

"You're not authorized to look at them sir." Grabbing his fat ass across the counter, I put my lighter to his face.

"Nigga I will burn this bitch down. I asked you to show me the tapes and I won't ask again." When I let him go, he reached for the phone. Quick pulled his gun and pointed it at him.

"I promise you don't wanna do that my nigga. Just take us to the back and show us the tapes. You get to go home and sleep tonight. Don't try to be the hero." He knew what Quick was saying and motioned for us to come to the back.

"Don't think about calling this in after we leave either. I will find you and I will melt your fucking skin off your body." The man nodded and showed us the footage. Out of nowhere, Shadow gave his ass a one two combo that put the nigga to sleep.

"Don't look at me like that, when he wakes up our black asses and the tapes will be gone." Focusing back on the tapes, I noticed the guy behind Drea.

"He was following her from the time she walked in the store. How the fuck you didn't realize someone was behind you?"

"Nigga it's a grocery store, somebody always behind you." Everything she said kept making sense, but I didn't want it to. I needed somebody to blame and I didn't want it to be me. As soon as Drea turned her back, he grabbed her and headed out the store.

"So we know it was one of the niggas that came to the house, when Drea left some other niggas showed up at the door. When I turned them down, they must have given him the okay to snatch her. How long did dude say he needed to find them?"

"He told me he would get back to me as soon as possible. I'm gone hit him up and let him know what the fuck just went down."

"In the meantime, I think we all need to move into the main house. We need everybody to be around each other. That's the only way to protect everybody at the same time." I agreed with Quick because being in my house would only drive me crazy.

"Hold the fuck up, only way I will agree to this shit if Blaze promise to leave the bullshit at his house." Shadow must be still pissed.

"He been cool lately, he should be straight."

"Baby Face are you smoking dog food? This nigga just threw shit on my wife and set it on fire. This nigga is aggy as ever." They looked at me in disbelief.

"Aight damn, I promise to leave yall weak ass alone. Now let's go, we gotta find my daughter. Heading to my car, Drea walked on the side of me looking stupid.

"Did you really do that girl like that."

"Fuck yeah and you need to be worried about your damn self. You two seconds away from getting your ass fucked up. Meet me at the fucking house so we can grab some clothes." Once I was away from everybody, I broke the fuck down. My baby girl was missing because I let my ego get in the way. All the playing and talking shit done got my baby kidnapped. One thing I know, it's gone be hell to pay when I find them.

CHAPTER 13- BABY FACE

This shit was getting crazier by the minute, but I refused to let mother fuckers come in and hurt my family. I'll put myself on the front line before that shit go down. Heading to my crib, I called my boy to make some shit happen.

"Jermaine what it do nigga."

"I'm still working on it. My guys are busting they ass to find these niggas. You didn't give me much to go on. It can't be that many cartels being ran in Puerto Rico."

"Put a rush on it, I'll pay extra. Listen, when we go out there we gone need a spot to stay. I need you to buy us some property there. Can you handle that for me?"

"I got you. You called me because you know I can make it happen. Just give me a couple days at the max. I'm gone try to get it to you sooner though. Stay out of sight until then, I can't have my friend getting into some shit."

"We got that handled. I'm waiting on your call." Hanging up the phone, I called Juicy mom and told her that I wouldn't be coming to get Zaria until I handled some shit. That was the last

thing I needed was my baby to get caught up in this bullshit. I can

only imagine how the fuck Blaze was feeling. The nigga was like

me in a lot of ways and I know he over there blaming his self.

Running in the house, I grabbed some shit, but I didn't

need much because me and my brothers always kept shit at the

main house. Jumping in my Hummer, I headed over prepared to

calm my family down. I know they needed me to keep them strong

in this situation.

Everybody would be panicking and me being the oldest, I

needed to keep shit in order. When I pulled up, I saw my brother's

cars were there and I walked in. As much as I hated the situation, it

was gone feel good to be around they ass. With the shit I had going

on with Juicy, I needed to be around family. When I walked in, it

was total chaos.

"What the fuck is going on?"

"The girls feel like Blaze shouldn't be allowed to bring his

lighters in here and you know what he saying." I got where the girls were coming from, but at the end of the day that's who Blaze was.

"Look, that nigga been the same for twenty six years. He ain't gone ever change and yall gone have to get over it. Everybody in this room has been burned by this nigga. Just don't do shit to piss him off. We not here for the bullshit and we got real life shit going on.

This man daughter has been kidnapped and yall sitting here arguing about some fucking lighters. Let his ass be great. Fire calms him, if you take the lighters you are creating a monster. This nigga done had a lighter since he could hold one, no bitch on this earth gone change my brother.

If you that scared, call up your families and go stay there. This is his house and you will not disrespect him in it. Get the fuck over it, or get the fuck gone."

"That's what the fuck I'm talking about nigga. Boss up on they ass. Fuck they think this is."

"Blaze shut up, the only reason Baby Face taking up for your ass is because he praying you don't light his ass up." I looked over at Shadow and the look I gave him let him know I was dead ass.

"You know when I'm serious nigga. Get your girl in check and leave him alone. He needs us right now and I won't allow anyone make him feel a certain kind of way in his shit."

"I appreciate the fuck out of you Face, but don't be talking like they got a nigga shook or some shit. If they know what's best, they would shut the fuck up." A nigga couldn't even take up for this simple mother fucker. Kimmie got up and rolled her eyes at Blaze. She was gone be a problem if she didn't fix her attitude. Nothing I could do would keep him from cremating her ass.

"Walk pass me again and roll your eyes. I promise I will set your big ass calves on fire. You probably want me to. They say heat and sweat makes you lose weight, you want me to melt them bitches in half sis?"

"Fuck you." He laughed and everybody went their separate ways. This mansion was big as fuck and had four different wings. I'm sure they could make it without being under each other. Walking out back, I stood there with so much on my mind.

"Bro, we gotta get her back. That's my world man."

"I know, we gone get her. You have to trust me even if I have to give my life to save hers, she coming home."

"I said the same shit to Drea. No matter what, my baby girl was gone be straight."

"Yall niggas out here holding hands and shit. Fuck yall doing." Turning around, I saw Shadow and Quick had come out as well.

"Nigga you better get Kimmie ass under control. Blaze gone fuck that girl up, I don't know why people insist on trying him. This the pettiest nigga in the fucking world. You would think she knows that by now."

"I be trying to tell her ass. If she wanna poke the bear that's on her. Bro, just know I ain't in that shit. A nigga got perfect eyebrows, I ain't trying to lose my shit." This nigga Shadow was terrified of Blaze.

"She lucky I gave my word or I would be thinking of some shit to do as we speak. Too much on my mind. Oh, let me show yall my new toy I got. Hold on." We looked at this nigga like he was crazy, but he ran off and we just stood there in our own thoughts. This nigga came back out the door with a mother fucking flame thrower. He had that shit on his back looking like he was ready for war.

"Nigga where the fuck you carrying that big ass mother fucker?" Quick was laughing, but he looked scared as hell.

"I'm about to try this mother fucker out." When he turned and aimed it, I moved the fuck back. This nigga Blaze with a flame thrower, issa Cajun. As soon as he pulled the trigger, that fire shot out so fast, it caught Quick in the ass. Shadow pulled out his phone and started recording while Quick ran his dumb ass in the pool and jumped in.

"My bad bro, I didn't know it shoot that far. For your name to be Quick, you move slow as hell my nigga."

"Nigga you set my ass cheeks on fire. The fuck." Me and Shadow had tears in our eyes we were laughing so hard.

"Yall gotta see the video. This nigga whole ass was really on fire." When Shadow hit play, I couldn't breathe I was laughing so hard.

"I'm glad yall think this shit funny. How the fuck I'm supposed to lay down with crispy cheeks?"

"Nigga you better lay down on your side. For real though, get some sleep. We don't know when this nigga gone call us with the info. We have to be ready." They all nodded in agreeance and we walked back in the house.

"I'm trying to figure out why the fuck I had to climb off my dick to come sleep with yall raggedy asses?"

"Ma, straight up we don't wanna hear that shit. Go lay your old ass down somewhere and why the hell you got Devon here when you knew what the hell was going on?"

"Ain't shit old on me and I'm your mama I can say what the fuck I want." We didn't respond to her bullshit, I looked over at the pastor and waited for him to answer. When he didn't, I asked again.

"Devon, can you explain to me why you are here. At this point, I don't trust no mother fucker and you dating my mama. She ain't shit and you a pastor so what's your motive."

"Nigga you tried it. Don't play pussy and get fucked. He here because I want him here." Moving her to the side, I looked at Devon again.

"Now that you mention it, his old ass do look like he could be mixed or some shit." Blaze ass pointed his flame thrower at him and I didn't stop him. I needed answers.

"Your mama told me what was going on and I wanted to pray for you all."

"Nigga I wish your ass would bring that churchy shit in here. You won't make it out of here. I talk to God on my own that's my nigga."

"Blaze your ass going to Hell." I agreed with Shadow, he didn't give a shit what he said.

"It's ok, you know how much fire in that mother fucker." Shaking my head, I walked off.

"See yall in the morning. This too much." I was gone let Devon make it tonight, but he better pray he legit. When I got upstairs, I laid down, but I was restless. Too much shit was on my mind and the only thing that would fix that was some pussy.

Grabbing my phone, I called Royalty.

"What you on?"

"Shit, laying down. What you want?"

"Some of that pussy, now bring it here."

"I'm on the way."

"I'll meet you there." Hanging up the phone, I eased out the house without anybody noticing. She was fine, but we don't bring strangers to the main house. That's why I'm pissed at my mama. I'm gone have my guy look into this pastor. I don't trust his ass, but in the meantime, I'm about to go balls deep in some much needed pussy. Stopping by the store, I made sure I grabbed a condom.

CHAPTER 14- QUICK

Walking to the pool, I was finally able to do some shit. When Blaze sat my ass on fire a few days ago, I could barely sit my ass down. The shit wasn't funny, but every time I walked pass these simple mother fuckers they were laughing and cracking jokes. The water felt good hitting my ass and I was enjoying the peace by myself.

"Baby, why didn't you tell me you were getting in the pool?" Ash was standing there looking good as hell, she barely gained any weight during this pregnancy. Zavi had already jumped in the water, so Ash came in as well. The way she walked over to me for some reason was sexy as hell. We hadn't been on good terms since I killed that nigga Jason, which means a nigga ain't been getting pussy. As soon as she was close enough, I grabbed her and pulled her to me. Looking over her shoulder, I made sure Zavi wasn't paying us any attention. Picking her up around my waist, I moved her swim suit to the side.

106

"Baby what are you doing? My stomach too big for this and our son is in the pool with us."

"Did I ask you for permission?" She shook her head no. "This my pussy right?" She bit her lip and nodded yes. "Then ride this dick. Before she could respond, I slid inside of her. She couldn't avoid the moan that came out of her mouth. Easing her body up and down on my dick slowly, I was trying not to make it look obvious. She leaned down and bit my lip and I lost it. Easing my dick in her, I started pushing harder. My dick was brick hard and this shit wasn't working.

"Zavi, do your pops a favor and go in the house and make me some kool aid."

"Okay daddy, I'll do it all by myself." As soon as he was out the pool and in the house. I let her down and pushed her against the wall. Spreading her legs, I slammed my dick back inside her. The water and her juices was giving my dick a vibration and the shit felt good as fuck.

"Damn girl, I love this pussy." The louder she moaned the harder my dick got. Grabbing her by her ass, I rammed my shit in as far as it could go and we both screamed out at the same time.

"Daddy, I'm cumming."

"Me too ma. Fuck." My nut shot out of me and my knees got weak. This was why my ass was so sprung on her ass. She had the best pussy in the world.

"You mother fuckers nasty as fuck." When we looked up, my brothers were standing there looking at us.

"Shut up, why the fuck yall watching anyway?"

"Nigga that shit was looking good as hell and the sounds had me ready to go knock Drea's back out."

"You ain't got no home training nigga." Agreeing with Baby Face, I put my dick up and kissed my girl. I'm not ashamed for being on some exotic shit fucking my wife.

"Bring your bleached dick ass on. We got a location." When I heard Shadow say that, I jumped out the pool quick as hell. Running upstairs, I showered and got dressed. As soon as I walked back into the room, Ash was there crying.

"I don't want you to go."

"Baby you know I have to. It's either all four of us or none of us. You know how we roll. If it was Zavi, they would be there for me. Don't put me in the position to choose."

"Don't worry, I'll never do that. You would never pick me over your brothers."

"That's the thing, my brothers would never ask me to. You're my wife and the mother of my child, your well being will always come first. Just know that this affects us all."

"Just come back safely. We need you."

"I got you baby. You know I'm coming back, I need some more of that fye ass pussy." Kissing her, I walked out the door and went to give Zavi a hug. After everyone said their good byes, we headed to the airport.

"Face, did you make sure the plane was fueled up? A nigga ain't trying to go down in that bitch before we get there?"

"Nigga we good, we even got a place to stay. I bought us some property. When have you ever known me not to be thorough?"

"Man, I'm just trying to make sure we come back in one piece. What about weapons?"

"Already taken care of. Nigga just be ready. You were rusty the last time you pulled the trigger. We can't have any mistakes out here."

"Fuck you nigga. I'm good." By the time we got to the airport, everyone was quiet in their own thoughts. This would be fucked up if we made it through all that shit back home and get here for it all to end. We could not let this go bad.

****

Walking into the house, we got situated then met back downstairs to come up with a plan. We couldn't just go in there and get our ass lit up.

"Jermaine gave us a layout of the estate, but a nigga going off memory. We don't know where they are holding Spark, so we have to proceed with caution until we have her. Once we get her, nothing else matters. Get the fuck out of there and make sure we all make it out. Kill anybody that gets in your way. Are we clear?"

"Yeah nigga. You could have kept that we didn't land on Plymouth Rock ass speech. We familiar my nigga." Baby Face was always going into some long drawn out ass speeches.

"Blaze your ass better take some guns and not that lil ass lighter why you talking shit."

"Light these nuts. Let's go get my baby girl and get the fuck out of here." We strapped up and headed out. I'm not gone lie, a nigga was nervous as fuck. We never took on an entire Cartel before and it was only four of us. Trying not to think negative about the situation, I started playing with my nine. Out of all the guns I used, it was my favorite. Shadow had been quiet since we left the main house and it was bothering me.

"Baby bro what's on your mind?"

"This shit just don't feel right. We going to their shit and we walking in there four deep. We supposed to be out this life and here we are again with our life on the line."

"I feel you lil nigga, but you a mother fucking Hoover. You may never be completely out this shit and you have to be okay with that. We lived a life and did some things that created some enemies along the way. Just because we done don't mean they are. We have always come out on top and we always will. Our bloodline won't let us lose." Nodding in agreement with Blaze, I went back to cleaning my shit. When we pulled up, I looked at the only niggas in the world that had my back and I knew we would be okay. Plus, nobody was colder at this gun play than me. I only know one other nigga and he retired. Stepping out, we looked at each other and headed into what could possibly be our last hurrah.

CHAPTER 15- BLAZE

The entire time, I tried to play this shit cool. To be honest, this was the first time I was actually scared of something. Don't get shit twisted, I'm not scared of no nigga that walked this mother fucker like I did, but I didn't know if my baby was still alive or if I would make it out with her. She didn't deserve this shit and it was fucking with me.

Everybody keep making these cracks like my lighter ain't shit, but niggas have feared me for twenty years behind this Bic. My gun play was serious, but the things I could do with fire was ridiculous. They can talk that shit, but my lighter can do just as much damage. Even though I wanted to burn they fucking flesh off, this was not that type of situation. A nigga needed to be on point and remember that I can't use fire this time.

Too many thoughts were running rapid in my mind and a nigga was trying to keep busy. Everybody always looked at me as the strong one that don't give a fuck, so nobody really checked to see how I was actually doing behind this shit. A nigga was hurting

113

bad, but I promise I will die before I leave my baby with these fuckers. Only thing I was scared of was Baby Face easing his pretty ass back to the states and fucking my bitch again. When the car stopped, I knew I had to get my shit together in order to pull this shit off. Stepping out, I looked at this big ass estate and got discouraged.

"Nigga how in the fuck are we supposed to know where to look in this big ass house?" Baby Face didn't say we were coming to a mini fucking Island.

"I told you he said he didn't know where she was. We just have to look."

"If we make it pass the gate and into the fucking house, we don't know where to look. We have no idea what part of the house my baby girl is in." As soon as I said that, a room on the downstairs floor was on fire. "Nigga let's go. If Spark is my child and ready pussy didn't play my ass, she set that room on fire."

"Let's go." Making sure our silencers were on, we hopped the gate and took out the first line of security. Actually Quick did, by the time I raised my gun they were hitting the ground. Heading into the house, Shadow and Baby Face took out the next set of

guards. I ran straight for the room that was on fire. When I walked

in the door, Spark was choking from the smoke and a candle was

knocked over. Who the fuck lights candles in a room with a

toddler. Grabbing her, I walked out the room with tears in my eyes.

She was okay and I could take her home. Looking up, a man across

the room was standing there smirking with his gun pointed at me.

Kissing my baby girl, I turned my back and held her as tight as I

could. There was no way I was letting one of the bullets hit her. I

would take them all for my baby.

"Never forget that daddy loves you baby."

"Me love Da Da." Smiling with tears falling down my face,

I closed my eyes. Hearing his gun go off, I braced myself for the

hit. A body fell against me and I turned to see what happened.

Baby Face was laying there choking on his blood. Fuck. He must

have jumped in front of the gun fire to save me and Spark. Quick

came through the front and aired the man out. Shooting him at

least ten times, he was dead and no longer a threat.

"Face, what the fuck man. Why did you do that?"

"Yall get out of here. Make sure she gets home safe. I had to protect you. I love you niggas."

"Nigga naw, get up. Face you have to get up." When his eyes closed, my heart shattered. Passing the baby to Shadow, I grabbed Face and threw him over my shoulder.

"Quick, shoot anything that moves. No nigga can out shoot you. I need you to be all of us right now and lay they ass down."

"You know I got you bro, let's go." Running towards the door, Quick was shooting niggas left and right, but they were still coming. Barely making it to the car, I shot out of there like a bat out of hell. I put the closest hospital in the GPS and headed there.

"Call our doctor and tell him to get on the next plane out. If Face pull through we can't let him stay at their hospital. He will be dead by morning." Quick grabbed his phone and made the call. As soon as we pulled up, I grabbed Face and rushed him inside. The nurses came running towards us and the put him on the stretcher. They checked him and started spitting out orders.

"No pulse, get him to the OR stat. Let's go people we have a code blue." Walking over to Shadow, I grabbed Spark and cried as I held her. My brother may have died to save us and that shit

was hurting a nigga soul. Sitting there silently, I sat in my own

guilt until a doctor came out four hours later to talk to us.

"It was touch and go for a while. He coded a few times, but

we were able to get the bullet out that was cutting an artery. We

repaired it and he is stable. He will be in a lot of pain and probably

out of it until tomorrow, but he is fine."

"Thank you for saving my brother Doc." Finally able to

breathe, I sat down and thanked God for keeping my brother. This

war was far from over and this was the first time I felt like we

wouldn't make it out.

****

After sneaking Face out of the hospital, we took him to the

house and our doctor was there waiting on him. Hooking him up to

the IV and a heart monitor we stole from the hospital, it was as if

he never left. He just needed to heal. When he opened his eyes the

next day, I could fully relax my mind.

"Bro you good?"

"Yeah, but the shit hurt like hell."

"Don't ever do that shit again. You have a baby at home and she needs you. I know you were looking out for me, but that shit would have ended a nigga. You the only father we know and we need your ass."

"You baby girl need you too. Plus, you already died once nobody would have believed your ass was gone for real this time. You can't be around here faking deaths and shit."

"I'm just glad you okay. We the fucking Hoover Gang it's all of us or none of us." I looked at Shadow like he lost his mind.

"Nigga yall ain't die with me fuck out of here. That only work when we robbing banks and shit. I'm not killing myself if one of yall go. You got me fucked up, ain't no pussy in Hell. I died before and the shit wasn't that great."

"Why you niggas can't be serious for once. This shit is fucked up." Quick had a point, but hell laughing was good for the soul when everything in your life was going fucked up.

"Yall know this shit is far from over right?" Everybody got silent and I knew they agreed. "It's too many of them and this is a war we may not win."

"It's a war I'm not willing to lose. These niggas tried to kill you while you were holding your daughter. I damn near died and I'm not stopping until somebody dead." Baby Face was dead set on going to war.

"Nigga that somebody gone be our ass. We can't go up against they ass. We not deep enough. We barely made it out."

"We just gone have to keep breaking they ass down. They lost some soldiers today and if we keep hitting them they will lose more and more."

"Your decision is to go to war?" He nodded and I could see the fear on Shadow's face. "You know what that means then right?"

"What's that?"

"We have to make a call. We need to call Lucifer."

CHAPTER 16- GANGSTA

"I can't wait to get you upstairs. From the print in your pants, I can tell you have a big long black dick." Smirking, I picked her up around my waist.

"You have no idea, now shut the fuck up you doing too much talking."

"Damn daddy, I like that rough shit." Grabbing her around her neck, I squeezed as hard as I could without snapping it.

"What the fuck did I say? If you say another fucking word, you're gonna piss me off and trust me you don't want that." Walking up the stairs, I laid her down on the bed. "Since you like it rough, give me something to tie you up with." She reached in her drawer and gave me three neck ties. I'm guessing they were her husband's.

"Damn, I forgot my condoms give me a second." Running to my car, I grabbed my bag and headed back in. She was still laid in the same spot, but was now playing in her pussy. "Did I tell you to start without me? I see you think you can do what the fuck you

120

want, but that shit about to change. Taking her hands, I tied her

wrists to the headboard. Taking the last tie, I gagged her with it.

The anticipation in her eyes was obvious. She wanted a nigga bad,

but I wanted her more. Sitting on top of her, I licked my lips and

her eyes begged me to stop teasing her. Raising my hand, I stroked

her face with the back of my hand.

In one swift motion, I punched her in her throat. Her eyes

bulged out of her head and the look of confusion filled her eyes.

Placing my hand over her mouth and nose, I took the remaining air

that she had and watched as she took her last breath. Once I was

satisfied she was gone and wouldn't be able to scream, I got up and

grabbed my pocket knife. Slicing an entry point all over her body, I

took the knife and started peeling her skin off.

When I had her entire face gone and the skin off her body

was removed, I grabbed my pliers. Pulling each tooth out of her

mouth, I packed up all of the remains and left just as quietly as I

came. When I jumped in my rental, I drove off feeling satisfied.

Waiting until I was about ten miles away from the scene, I let my

window down and removed my gelled on finger prints. Tossing her remains, I was ready to go. Heading back to the private plane, I

jumped on and reflected over the day events. Paradise had no idea

where I was and I intended to keep it that way. A nigga supposed

to be retired, but every now and then I take on a job. Going from

the highest paid hitman and most feared killer to husband and

father was a hard transition for me.

I promised my wife and brother I would stay out the game,

but I couldn't. This shit was in my DNA and I felt like life was

passing me by. Something about peeling the flesh off a mother

fucker gave me a rush like no other. After the shit with Journey, I

promised to never cheat on my girl again. When a nigga take on a

hit, I make sure I don't actually give these bitches the dick, but I

sell them a dream in order to get in their world.

Just in case mother fuckers didn't know who I was, I had

no problems letting them know. I was Kenneth "Gangsta" Jamison.

Known to most people as The Devil or Lucifer. I picked up that

name after the world realized the way I preferred to kill. My

brother Suave had that same monster inside of him and he can be sick when he wanted to be. The difference was he only killed when he had to, I did it for sport.

Well we used to. Now days, all we do is have play dates with the kids or trips with our wives. I needed to kill like I needed to breathe. I'm not gone sit here and reflect on my entire life or how I got this way. That's why I agreed to let Latoya Nicole write my story. I thought it was dope how she titled it Gangsta's Paradise. Her ass did such a great job, Suave allowed her to do him and Tank's story. I don't know why she picked that dumb ass title No Way Out, but the story came out dope as fuck. She mastered that shit and covered every part of our life, but I didn't like how people walked up to me and thought they knew me.

I was a different type of nigga than people were used to. I'm stupid dumb wicked with a gun. It would only take me seconds to lay down a room full of niggas, but I preferred to torture people. My thrill came from cutting niggas up and removing tongues and shit. Realizing that life is behind me now, I look forward to the random jobs I get. I don't know what this bitch did to her husband, but he paid me a million dollars to make sure they couldn't identify

her. The ride was quick since I was coming from Miami.

My brother convinced me to come out to Hawaii and live

with him and his family. When he retired from the drug game, he

relocated there. I still don't see how he gave all that shit up. He

was the biggest King Pin Chicago had ever seen and he walked

away from it all. When I ask him do he miss it, he always give me

some politically correct ass answer. He could tell that shit to

somebody else, but I knew him and I know that he wouldn't

choose this life if it wasn't for his family. Jumping into my

Maserati GT I headed home and made it my business to be quiet as

hell as I snuck in the shower. Climbing into bed with my wife, I

woke her up because I needed some pussy. No one can get my dick

harder than a dead body. The rush I feel after a kill, takes me to

different heights. Sliding in between her legs, I sucked hard

enough to wake her up. My sex is always aggressive after a kill.

Flipping her legs back, I slapped her hard as hell on her ass causing

her to wake up. The best thing about Paradise was, she never

turned me down when it came to sex. Slapping her across her

124

pussy, she moaned and reached for my dick. Snatching her up by her hair, I flipped her over and pushed her head down in the bed.

"Spread your ass cheeks open." As usual, she did as she was asked. Watching my dick slide in her pussy, a nigga couldn't help but moan. I've had my share of bitches, but my wife had the best pussy in the world. Slamming my dick into her none stop, she took that shit and threw that ass back. Feeling my nut rise, I pulled out.

"Come catch this nut." Barely able to turn around after the punishment I just put on her pussy, she opened her mouth. Grabbing her by her head, I fucked her face until my nut shot down her throat. Pulling out, I laid down. "I love you girl."

"I love you more G." And her ass was back sleep.

****

"Baby, wake up Suave here and want to talk to you." Groaning, I rolled over and looked at the time. It was one in the afternoon, so I got my ass up and handled my hygiene. When I walked down stairs, he was sitting in my office.

"What's up big bro?"

"Where have you been going in the plane?"

"Damn nigga, at least speak when you walk in my house."

"What's up baby bro, now tell me where the fuck you been going?"

"On trips for my business. Why, what the fuck is the problem?"

"The problem is your ass is lying. Nigga you been doing jobs and I told you that shit is dead. You said you were leaving that life behind. We almost didn't make it out the last time." Him and Paradise both used that over my head when they wanted to keep me on board. Paradise was the heiress to the Garzon Cartel and we had to take out her punk ass father. They keep saying we barely made it, but we did. Took out their entire organization and the only mother fucker we left behind was her mama and the dog. This nigga act like we still got enemies out here and shit.

"Look, that's a part of me. In order for me to stay out of that life is to indulge in it here and there. I be needing a fix."

"I'm gone fix the plane on your ass and you ain't gone make it back next time. Keep playing with me nigga."

"That was almost convincing, a nigga damn near believe your ass." Our laughing was cut short when my phone rung. Looking at the number, I knew something had to be wrong. He hadn't called me in years. Looking at Suave, I gave him the something is up face.

"The fucking world must be ending if this nigga Blaze calling me. What up boi."

"Nigga you don't fuck with me, Baby Face your nigga."

"Yeah you right, your ass play too much and I'll be done fucked your ass up. What's up though, you hitting me up for a reason."

"Long story short, my daughter was kidnapped and Baby Face got shot up trying to save us. We all made it out and we good, but the war ain't over. It's too many of them to go up against and we need your help. We need Lucifer, I know you retired and all but we need you."

"I'm on the way."

CHAPTER 17- SUAVE

This nigga Gangsta thinks he slick. The log in at the airport showed him leaving in the plane once a month. He knew we gave that shit up. The way the shit was going, our ass would be dead if we kept moving in the same way. I was a calm subtle nigga and I wasn't into wars and shit. My name spoke volumes and all that rah rah shit wasn't me. My world literally got flipped upside down when I met my wife Tank.

Not only did she get a nigga to settle down, she also came with a lot of baggage and a war that wasn't mine. I was retired when G needed my help with the cartel, but I'm done. Almost losing my wife changed my perspective. Having more money than I could count, a nigga didn't need to still be out here in these streets. Not to mention my girl and her crew think they hittas like us. Climbing out of bed, I got up to go holla at my brother. I needed to know what he was into and if it could affect us all.

"Where you going baby?"

"I'm going to holla at Gangsta for a minute. I'll be back in a few. Have me some food done and be naked when I get back."

"You don't give this pussy a break."

"You want me to give this dick to somebody else?"

"I gave up the street shit because you asked me too, but I still got my heat don't make me use it."

"What did I tell you about threatening me? Check your tone before I check it for you." She looked at me crazy, but she shut her ass up. I was Kendyl "Suave" Jamison. The biggest King Pin the Chi ever saw, but I left it behind for her. Even when I was in the streets, I never raised my voice. I didn't have to do all that. When I spoke, mother fuckers knew I meant business.

Throwing on my clothes, I headed out and went to my brother's spot. He only stayed five minutes from me, so I did my daily jog over. When he walked in the door, I knew he was about to lie to me. After finally getting him to tell me the truth, I got where he was coming from. Hell, I missed the shit all the time, but it was about priorities. That ain't our scene anymore. I left it all to my nigga Smalls and I made money sitting back relaxing. It's been a couple years since I even fired a gun.

Realizing it was Blaze on the phone, I knew it couldn't be good. Face ran with us back in the day, but he had his own crew. They didn't have friends it was just his brothers The Hoover Gang. Not being able to hear what he was saying, I hoped Gangsta put the call on speaker, but he didn't.

"I'm on the way." When he hung up the phone, he turned to me and I knew in that moment, we were going back into the life.

"Where you going G?"

"You mean we nigga. If I go to war, I need to know the person I trust most is on the battle field with me."

"You trying to get me divorced? Hell, are you trying to piss off Paradise?" She was the only person I knew that was sick like my brother. He would never admit it, but he was scared of her ass.

"You know damn well we don't have a choice in the matter. They like family and we can't leave them out there like that. They kidnapped Blaze daughter and shot up Face. They still coming for them and they need us."

"Who is they?"

"Nigga I don't know shit. He said they so I'm saying they. All I know is it's a Cartel in Puerto Rico. We will get all the details when we get there. We at least have to go to hear them out and find out what the fuck is going on." Running my hand over my face, as much as I wanted to say no we couldn't. We didn't live by that code. They knew we were retired and the fact that they still called, it has to be bad.

"If we do this, we can't leave for a couple of days."

"They could be dead in a couple of days."

"Nigga we could be dead if we don't try and butter our wives up first. I'll call Smalls and have him and his crew keep an eye on them until we get there."

"You scared of Tank ass huh?"

"Don't get beat the fuck up, you know damn well I ain't scared of shit. Get fucked up if you want to."

"We ain't kids no more, I will lay your ass out."

"Lay on deez nuts."

"I don't play that gay shit bro. Pull that shit out if you want to. I'll cut that shit off and feed them bitches to your wife and tell her it's hard boiled eggs." Standing up, I walked in his face.

"What you saying nigga? All this talking you doing ain't moving me."

"Sit your old ass down. Fuck around and have a stroke if I sneeze on your ass." He laughed, but G knew not to fuck with me. He learned everything he knew from me, that nigga knew what it was and didn't want these problems.

"Do something special for your girl before she beat your ass."

"Aight bro. Holla at me with the specific time." Leaving his house, I decided to make my call before I got home. Tank was going to go the fuck off and most importantly, she was gone try to go with me. Not this time around, I didn't know what we were up against and I wasn't having that shit. Dialing Smalls, I needed him to look out for the fam.

"What up nigga. Is something wrong with the payment? I counted that shit myself so it should be good."

"Naw it's straight, I know you legit. I need you to do me a favor. You know The Hoover Gang right?"

"Yeah, I remember them from back in the day. You were close to the oldest brother."

"Yeah, he needs my help and it looks like me and G are back in the game until we help them out of this situation. I need to smooth this shit over with Tank, so I need you to make sure they straight until I get there."

"Say no more. You know I got your back and when you get here count me and my crew in. Whatever it is, it don't matter. Shit been boring around here anyway."

"You sound like G ass. This nigga been sneaking and doing hits."

"I don't think you thought about the real problem you gone have."

"What's that?"

"Nigga Blaze and Gangsta in the same room. I don't even know Blaze all that well, but he disrespectful and ignorant as fuck. Nigga will set anybody on fire."

"That's his nigga they gone be straight, but it is gone be funny as fuck to see. On some serious shit though, make sure you have the crew ready. We trying to be in and out that bitch. I don't need Tank ass coming down there on no rah rah shit."

"Yall talk that good shit, but she done saved your life a couple of times. My bitch the one that can't fight. Bald head ass can't even fight the perm on her edges right. I ain't never seen a mother fucker with hair that nap up a few hours after they get a perm. I be begging her ass to get a sew in. She talking about she going natural. Look like I married a fucking sea monkey."

"Nigga you ignorant, I can't wait to see your ass."

"Gone head on with that soft shit. Shoot me the info and I'll see you in a couple of days." Hanging up the phone, I walked in the door and prepared to do some major ass kissing. This was gone take some finessing, but at the end of the day she had no choice but to roll with it. For some reason, now that I knew I was going to war, I was excited. Murder always got my blood moving.

CHAPTER 18- TANK

Rolling over in my bed, I thanked God for another day. He brought us out some shit and I was grateful for being given the chance to be with my family. Knowing Suave wanted food ready when I got home, I got my ass up and jumped in the shower. I knew not to play with him, he was one of those silent threats and killers. He was one of the sweetest people ever until you crossed him. In the beginning, we bumped heads a lot because he wanted me to quit acting like a street thug and be the mother to our child. That's who I was though, Lashay Wright a bitch from the streets. To keep a happy home, we both agreed to leave that shit in the past and raise our son. Kendyl Jamison, Jr. but we call him Deuce. Our big boy was now two years old. When Gangsta moved here, I thought it was going to be hell. That man scared me so bad if he walked in the room I got goose bumps. Over time, we grew close but he still has ways about him that shake my ass to the core. Having a baby changed him and Paradise. I've never met a couple that was equally sick in the head. Laughing at my own joke, I went in the kitchen and started making some steak, potatoes, and asparagus. Feeling my pussy jump, I knew he had walked up behind me. Turning around, I kissed him and sucked on his bottom lip.

"The food will be ready in a minute baby."

"Fuck that food, go get dressed I want to take you out." Looking in his eyes, I knew it was some bullshit in the game.

"You're not going back." If I didn't know anything else, I knew my husband. Even though he was calm and laid back all the time, he had a certain look in his eyes when he was about to kill somebody. Knowing he had no enemies here, that could only mean one thing.

"What did I tell you about demanding some shit with me. I'm the nigga and you my wife. Act like it."

"NO YOU ACT LIKE IT. How could you make that decision without talking to me first? You just said I'm your wife, then I should have a say so."

"It's not for good, I just have to go help my people. It won't take long."

"How many times have we been through this? We barely made it out the last two. You have a child to live for and I'm not about to let you go and possibly get hurt over somebody else shit."

"Loyalty means everything to me and I need you to understand there are some people in my life I have to be there for no matter what. If something happened to Smalls or Nik, do you think I would sit here and not do shit?"

"I get what you are saying, but the minute you said I do and had a child, we became your top priority."

"Lashay you are wasting your breath. This is not negotiable baby. I'll be back soon." Walking up to my face, I knew he was about to threaten me. His eyes went cold.

"Hear me well. If you even think about showing up, you won't have a husband when it's over. Stay here with our son and make sure he is good. I'll be back.

"You think I'm letting you go without me?"

"You heard what the fuck I said and I have never been in the business of repeating myself. Stay your ass here or lose me."

Walking away from him, I went in the room and slammed my door. This was the Suave that I didn't like.

A bitch and her crew was just as cold with the gun play as him and his boys. Hell, I saved his fucking life more than once. How could he even think about making me stay here? Grabbing my phone, I called Paradise.

"Hey sis, can you meet me at Starbucks? We need to talk."

"When?"

"Right now and don't tell Gangsta where you are going."

"Aight, but it better be good if you have this crazy mother fucker ready to fight me, it better be worth my while." Hanging up the phone, I put on my running gear and acted like I was going for a jog to clear my mind.

"Baby, keep an eye on Deuce. I need to clear my head so I'm going for a run."

"I got him, but don't play with me Lashay. Try me if you want to, I'm gone hurt your fucking feelings."

"Yes, massa I heard you. I'll be back." As soon as I got out the door, I took off running. Not trusting him, I didn't want him trying to follow me. When I walked in Starbucks, Paradise was already sitting there sipping on a frappe. Heading to the counter, I ordered me a Vanilla Bean frappe and sat down.

"Why you got me lying to Lucifer and sneaking out of the house and shit?"

"Has he said anything to you about going somewhere?"

"Naw he ain't said shit. Where the fuck he going?"

"Somebody need their help in Chicago, they going back to their old ways to help a mother fucker I don't even know. Then the nigga said if I try to pop up, he leaving me."

"Let me guess, you want me to go with you."

"Yes, the last time he went on his own without me, I almost lost him. I'm not going through that again."

"I'm a rogue bitch, so you know I don't mind going with you. All I ask is you really think this over and figure out if it's worth you losing your husband over. Suave is not the type of nigga that give idle threats. He the craziest of us all because he is the quiet before the storm. If you're willing to lose it all to save his life then I'm down."

"If he leaves me for making sure he good, then so be it. At least he will be alive to help raise our child."

"We have another problem. If they leave in the plane, how the fuck we gone get there and how we gone get our weapons through baggage?"

"Bitch we can fly commercial, we just gone go first class. My crew in the Chi will have weapons for us there. Let me worry about that, but please don't say anything to Gangsta. The only thing I need you to figure out is where they are going." She stood up from the table.

"I got you, but I gotta get out of here. A bitch might have to suck some toes or something for this info. You gone owe me bitch. Babysitting duties for six months."

"Damn bitch and your baby bad as hell. I never seen a one year old lil girl get into the shit that she does."

"Not my problem." Laughing, she walked out the door. Grabbing my phone, I called my crew.

"Guess what bitches. I'm coming home."

CHAPTER 19- PARADISE

After all me and my man had been through, married life was great. Me and G had been through the unthinkable, but it made our shit stronger. We were made for each other and had a bond like no other. Name another couple that enjoyed decapitating a nigga together. We were one in the same, but we gave all that up to be parents. Our daughter Kenya was one and I swear she was bad as hell. You could tell she had our genes and I prayed for whatever nigga was gone be her man.

Walking back in the house, it looked like a tornado hit it. My ass was only gone fifteen minutes, how the hell G let her do this shit that quick is beyond me. When I made it to bedroom, I could see how. His ass was knocked out and she was using a marker writing on my red bottoms. Somebody was about to die. This nigga done lost his damn mind, he knows our baby bad as fuck. Why would you go to sleep on her? He was already in the dog house. His ass thinks he slick because I ain't said shit, but I know he killed somebody last night. The only time G has sex like he trying to rip me open is after a hit. I wanted to give him a

chance to tell me his self, but the nigga walking around like it's

sweet. Most of the time, I let shit slide because of the guilt I always

feel. See, G was already a monster but I turned him into Lucifer.

Literally training him to be the hitman he was today, he throws it

in my face any time I want him to be normal. I was a young bitch

that wanted a nigga as crazy as me and I saw the potential in him.

I was Paradise Garzon and the daughter of Louis and Mary

Garzon head of the Garzon Cartel. Growing up, I was trained by

the best and I needed a nigga as crazy as me. When I saw the

monster that G possessed I knew I could mold him into the most

feared nigga to walk the streets. Teaching him to cut off feelings

and kill in such a way mother fuckers were scared to sleep at night.

He was Gangsta, but I turned that nigga into Lucifer himself.

When I got older, I wanted that nigga to show feelings and

emotions and he ain't have shit for a bitch. He has been working

hard to show me now that we are married, but I can tell it's still a

struggle for him. We both agreed to turn in our machetes for

bottles and diapers. His ass done reneged on that agreement. Now his ass planning on going back without me, he got me fucked up.

Tank was pissed, but I played it cool. Little did she know, I was

ready to kill his ass. Not for going back, but for leaving me behind.

How the fuck you gone be having a good time slicing niggas up

and I'm stuck at home changing shit diapers?

Not wanting G to slip back to the nigga he was and

completely turning into the devil, I would rather have the family

life. A bitch would be lying if I said I didn't miss the power

though. The feeling I got when I rode a nigga dick and sliced his

throat was like no other. When people look at us, they

automatically think he is the worse. That's far as fuck from the

truth, G ain't have shit on me and he knew it.

Grabbing my red bottoms that Kenya was writing on, I

slung it at his ass.

"Wake your ass up nigga."

"What the fuck Paradise. You be doing the most. A nigga

been letting you make it and you pushing me."

"Look at my fucking shoes. Why the hell would you go to

sleep on her knowing how bad she is?"

"Because I was fucking tired. Damn. You should have taken her with you."

"Tell me why you tired G." He got the dumbest look on his face and acted like he ain't hear me. Reaching down to pick up Kenya, he tried to play with her like we weren't in the middle of a conversation. "You heard me. Why the fuck is you tired G?"

"Shut the fuck up sometimes, damn. Your ass talk too fucking much. I'm tired because I am. Get the fuck out my face." As soon as he placed Kenya down, I ran up on him so fast he didn't have a chance to react. Charging his ass, he flew on the bed and I climbed on top of his ass in one swift motion. Before he could say anything else, I had my knife to his neck.

"What you not gone do is disrespect me because you don't want to tell your wife the fucking truth. We done been down this road and I be damned if I go back. If you ever disrespect me like that again, I will send your ass to your mama. Fuck with me if you want to." The adrenaline that rushed through me quickly faded when I saw his eyes change over. Looking into them bitches, it felt like I was looking right at the devil. All of his emotions were

144

turned off and I knew I was in for a fight. No matter how crazy and tough I was, this G scared me. Hell, it scared everybody. Before I could try to calm the situation, he grabbed the knife from me. I didn't even get the chance to fight to get it back, as soon as he snatched it my ass was on my back and he was on top of me.

"I told you before if you ever pulled another weapon on me, you better kill me." Grabbing me around my neck, he started choking all kinds of snot out my ass. My ass was getting dizzy and looking at him, I knew he wasn't going to let go. G was no longer here and Lucifer had now taken over.

Knowing my fate if my ass just laid here, I reached back and punched his ass so hard in his face his head snapped back. When he looked back into my eyes, his lip was bleeding. That nigga licked the blood and smirked and I prayed Jesus take the wheel. We were about to fight like two niggas in the street, but G was back. He had a spark in his eyes and they no longer looked dead.

He tossed the knife and punched my ass in the forehead. Who in the fuck does some shit like that? Feeling the knot rising, I leaned up and bit his lip. I tried to pull that mother fucker off until he pimp slapped my ass to the floor. Looking over at Kenya when I landed, this bad mother fucker was biting my shoes. If she wasn't one, I would have squared up with her ass. Getting off the floor, G was standing there waiting for me in his fighting stance. Swinging my arm at him to make him think I was trying to punch him, I brought my leg up and kicked his balls into his stomach. As soon as his ass bent over, I gave his ass an uppercut like that bus driver did that girl. I rocked his ass to the moon.

Doing a victory dance, I jumped up and down in a circle. By the time my ass turned back around, this nigga round housed my ass. It was a wax on wax off Karate Kid ass kick and I went soaring in the air. Thank God I landed on the bed.

Looking at him come at me, I tried to say "Gina iont wanna fight no more" in my Martin voice, but I think the nigga kicked my throat out. Feeling him snatch my pants off, the flood gates came open and he hadn't even touched me yet. As soon as his mouth hit my clit, I was cumming.

"Damn G suck that pussy baby." Trying to grab his hands, he snatched them back and pinned me down. He was winning the end of the fight by punishing my pussy with his tongue. A bitch came three times before he got up. When he put me in doggy style position, I knew he was about to beat my shit up. Grabbing my ass cheeks, he pulled them so far apart I felt the tip of my ass crack split like chapped lips. Knowing I couldn't do shit but enjoy this ride, I let him attack my pussy until I felt his body shaking.

"I love you girl."

"I love you too G." Rolling over, I kissed him. Grabbing our bad ass baby, I put her in her play pen and got in the bed. Both of our ass was out in seconds.

****

Waking up, I looked over and G was packing. My ass tried to stand up and it felt like my body had been run over by a train. How this nigga was moving around like it was nothing was beyond me.

"Where you going G?" I knew the answer, but he hadn't told me yet what was going on.

"Me and Suave gotta go back to Chicago. Don't trip, I should be back in a few days."

"What are yall going to do?" His body tensed up and I knew he didn't want to tell me that part.

"Look, I know we agreed to leave that part behind us but my people need me and I can't tell them no."

"Okay, why can't I go then? If it's as simple as you're trying to make it out to be, let's go handle this shit together."

"Not this time baby. I need you to stay here and keep an eye on Tank. Not to mention we have a child that you need to be here for."

"It's only one way I will agree to you leaving. You have to give me your exact location. If something happens and you don't return, I need to know where to come looking."

"I'm waiting on him to send me the location and I will give it to you. Thank you for not doing the most. Let a nigga be stressed free so I can come back and tear that pussy up."

"You know I'll be here waiting. I'll sleep with my legs open. Make sure you lick it first."

"Nasty ass. Let me get out of here. I'll text you the info in a few. If I'm not back in three days, come through that bitch killing anybody that's breathing. If my ass didn't make it they ain't either."

"Be safe baby and let me know when you make it." He leaned down and kissed me and walked out the door. That was easier than I thought it was gone be. Walking around the house, I cleaned up the mess Kenya made. Thinking about the shit I was about to pull gave me goose bumps. I couldn't wait to feel that rush again. The thought of cutting a nigga up had me excited. A bitch needed this shit.

CHAPTER 20- GANGSTA

Niggas didn't get the connection me and Paradise had. Fighting with her had my dick so hard, I thought the shit was gone bust. I'm not gone lie, when she pulled the knife on me her ass was about to go have a father daughter dance in the upper room. She knew I didn't play that shit. Her crazy is what turned me on the most. What other chick you know, you could have a fight like that and she ain't trying to call the police on your ass.

She wasn't weak and her ass was gone make sure the shit was an all out battle. When she upper cut my ass, that mother fucker almost knocked me to the moon. Seeing her do her happy dance pissed me off. My ass was standing there in my karate kid stand waiting on her to turn her ass around. That shit turned me on like a mother fucker.

Leaving out the house, my girl thinks she done played my ass. I knew her ass better than she knew herself. Paradise was my other half and I know what she thinks even when she don't say it. Her ass wants the address because she coming. Knowing Suave would be pissed, because Tank ass gone be mad as fuck I played

along. Truth is, my bitch more ruthless than damn near every thug

ass nigga I knew. I trusted her to have my back and make sure I got

my ass out alive. We killed together for ten years and I trusted her

with my life. When Suave found out, I'm gone play dumb as shit

and act like I didn't know her ass was coming.

Blaze sent me the info to his house in Chicago. They didn't

want the women to know that Baby Face had been shot and they

wanted him to heal before they went back. Everybody thinks they

still in Puerto Rico. We would try to get this handled as quickly as

possible before they figured anything out.

Sending the address to Paradise, I walked in Suave shit so

we could get there and go handle business.

"Bro, where you at? You ready?" When I ain't hear shit, I

pulled my gun out and walked quietly up the stairs. Hearing

someone muffled, it sounded like they had them gagged. Twisting

the knob slowly, I knew my ass only had a split second to access

the situation. When I opened the door, this nigga had Tank in some

type of swing shit hanging from the ceiling and her ass was tied up and gagged. Nothing about my sister turned me on, but this shit

looked interesting as hell. After watching for a couple more

minutes, I had enough.

"If you don't get your fifty shades of I can't fuck right ass

on and let's go."

"Nigga, get the fuck out." Tank was screaming something,

but I couldn't understand her since she was gagged.

"That's the best gift he ever gave your ass. Been telling his

ass since I met you that you talk too fucking much."

"G, give me ten minutes damn." Laughing, I walked out

and let them finish they freak session. She must have been really

acting up for her to agree to let him do that shit. When he finally

came out the room, I could tell he was irritated.

"Why the fuck you bust in my room like that?"

"Nigga I called out your name and I heard muffled

screams, I thought somebody got your ass. A nigga was trying to

save your life. Next time I'll let them kill your old ass."

"Fuck you. You got the address?"

"Yeah, we need to be in and out. I'm not trying to be there long or my ass ain't gone wanna leave."

"The streets have a way of sucking you back in. Let's go before she brings her ass in here crying again." Walking out the door, I wondered if he was just as excited as me.

"Big bro, you not a little excited about this shit? It's been a while since you had to fade a nigga." This nigga looked over his shoulder like Tank ass was in the car.

"Man, I miss this shit every day. A nigga getting too old to be out here dealing with all the problems the streets bring though. We got millions and I have no reason to still be out here taking risks, but I swear I miss the thrill of it all. I love my family, but I needed this excitement."

"That's why I take jobs here and there. This family life wasn't for me, but I'm doing it. I ain't gone lie though, it feels like a part of me is missing. Like I ain't being me, I'm pretending to be somebody else. My ass be dreaming about killing niggas and shit. My ass can be at the store and the person standing in front of me, I would stand there and think of ways to kill them. The shit driving

my ass crazy."

"You sound like your ass ready to say fuck the family life.

I'm proud of the nigga you became, but I get where you coming

from. It's hard, but you have to let that shit go. That ain't our life

no more G." Drifting away in my own thoughts, it seemed like

everybody got it, but nobody understood.

It feels like my ass is drowning or suffocating or some shit.

I needed to kill like I needed to breathe and mother fuckers was

asking me to let the shit go. How do you get something like that

out of your system? My entire identity was based around me being

the coldest killer niggas had ever seen. Feeling myself going into a

depressed state, I thought about the task at hand and immediately

got excited again. Loading the plane, I couldn't wait to land in

Chicago. Sending Smalls a text, I let him know to meet us at the

airport.

****

Looking at the house in front of us, these niggas had come

a long way. Blaze house was big as shit and the cars lined up in the drive way let me know they had made it. We all did good and it made a nigga proud to see how far we had come. Young black millionaires alive to tell the story.

"These niggas living like the rich and famous out this mother fucker." Smalls was admiring the house like I was. My shit was probably a little bigger, but this shit was nice.

"All us went way out with our houses, you the only nigga that got his shit built in the middle of the hood. I gave your ass the keys to the whole city and you out here living like you got a nine to five."

"Nigga I was born a hood rat and I'm gone die one. Fuck you mean. Don't front like you don't know what's in a niggas pockets."

"We know what's in them mother fuckers that's why we can't believe your ass trying to live ghetto fabulous. Get your ass out the hood. You don't eat where you shit nigga." Suave ass was always in lecture mode.

"Look, Malcolm X a nigga gone do what he wants. You picked your life and how you wanted to live and I chose mine. We both out here eating, I just choose to eat in the ghetto."

"Are we really gone stand out here and argue over houses? Bring yall dumb ass on." They about to get worked up over where a nigga choosing to lay his head. Ringing the bell, a dark skinned nigga answered the door. It must be they youngest brother, he the only one I ain't know like that. When he stood there blocking the door, it irritated me.

"Move the fuck out the way nigga."

"Who the fuck are you niggas and why are you here." This nigga lucky he they brother or he would have caught a fade quick.

"First off nigga, put a shirt on. You out here oily as shit in the middle of a fucking war. You ain't got time to take no pictures. Second, get the fuck on with all them fucking questions. You should already know who the fuck I am. My rep speaks for itself. Now you can play pussy and get fucked if you want to."

"G, calm down. He was too young to know who you are. Give the nigga a break." Suave was trying to calm the situation while Smalls ass just watched eating a bag of chips. Even after Suave said that shit, this nigga stared me down. He was about to learn a lesson today. In one swift motion, I had him pinned to the ground with my gun pointed at his head.

"Your attitude gone get your life cut short my nigga. Off the strength of your brothers, I'm gone let you make it. But I promise your ass better check your attitude quick or I'm gone forget who the fuck you are. Are we clear?" He was struggling under me, but I had his ass on lock. I knew he was pissed, but I don't allow any nigga to disrespect me.

"Gangsta, what the fuck is you doing nigga. This my little brother." Never taking my eyes off his ass, I responded to Blaze.

"You brother feeling tough today. I'm gone need you to explain to him who the fuck I am because this is the last time I'm gone let his ass be great." I heard a lighter and then saw the flame at my face.

"Nigga it's hard to be scared of a mother fucker with no eyebrows. Let his ass up before I leave your ass with a patchy eye my nigga."

"Blaze get that lighter out of my face before I make you swallow that bitch." When I felt the heat hit my face and heard my hairs sizzling, I pulled my gun away from Shadow's face.

"Aight damn. Get your lighter happy ass on before you have my shit looking like roasted peanuts."

"Get your dumb ass up and stop playing. He sensitive he ain't like us." Laughing, I stood up and reached my hand out to the lil nigga. When he didn't take it and tried to stand up on his own, I swooped his legs and he hit the floor again.

"By the time I leave, we gone have your attitude in check. Get out your feelings before I hurt them bitches." Stepping over him, we walked up the stairs to go holla at Baby Face.

"When you speak of the devil, he will appear. What the fuck took you so long nigga." Face looked weak, but other than that I can tell he was good. I'm glad they ain't fuck my nigga up.

"Man yall sent yall purse dog downstairs to open the door and I had to teach his ass some manners. This our nigga Smalls. Smalls this is Face, Blaze, Quick, and purse dog." I could tell the nigga wanted to say something smart, but he ain't wanna get

embarrassed again.

"Now that everybody here, what's the move? How are we

gone do this shit?" Even though me and Quick didn't really hang

like that, he was more like me. He was nice with his gun play as

well, but nobody was nicer than me.

"We know where the headquarters are, but we don't know

if that's it. We went in there and took out at least thirty niggas and

still barely made it out. They know where we live, but I don't think

they know about the main house. That's where we have everybody.

We either wait until they come here, but if we do that we won't

know if we got them all. Our ass will be like sitting ducks waiting

to see if more will come. So I say, we take the war to them. In

Puerto Rico." Thinking it over, I agreed with Baby Face.

"First off, fix your face lil nigga. You standing there in

your feelings and we here to save your fucking life. We gone all

need to work together and if I can't trust you to have my brother

back you considered an enemy. Now, we done been down this road before and it's hard to penetrate an estate from the outside unless we have the place surrounded.

My nigga Smalls will have his team with us, but they are not trained like us. We gone have to mix the crowd in order to make sure we don't have a weak side. Face, are you gone be good to go?" Suave was the only nigga I knew that could shake your soul without raising his voice. The lil nigga actually fixed his face after that.

"Whether I'm good or not, I'll be there. Me and my brothers never go without the other. It's either all of us or none of us. I know Shadow was too young and yall didn't hang around him, but at the end of the day that's my brother. Whatever happened downstairs, yall need to deaden that shit. Just like you protect yours, imma protect mine.

Now purse dog, get out your feelings. As he said, we needed them and they came out of retirement to help us. You may not personally know them, but you heard the stories of Lucifer and Suave. You are in the presence of legends. No man is going to take disrespect. We didn't bring them here to end up at war with they ass."

"Damn nigga you talk more than Suave ass. You can tell you the old nigga out the bunch. Yall got some food in this mother fucker? I can go eat a meal until yall niggas ready to talk about what we gone do. All this Kumbaya shit done made me hungry."

"The kitchen downstairs." Smalls left out after Quick told him where to go and we continued the conversation. We will catch him up later.

"Face, you just got shot days ago. How we gone go back right now?" I guess purse dog was out his feelings.

"Because if we wait we giving them the opportunity to come to us and that puts our family at risk. We were laying they ass out and it was only four of us and a baby. It's more of us now, we should be able to end this shit with no problem." I knew Quick laid most of them out by his self.

"Quick is the best nigga you know with a gun, but I'm better. I can lay out at least ten in five seconds. We got this, but we need a secure plan on how we are going in and who we are going

after."

"That's the thing. The nigga kept saying his boss, but we

don't know who that is. Our guy led us to the Cartel, but we don't

know who is actually in charge of it." Listening to everything

Quick was saying, going to war now may not be a good idea.

"That can pose as a problem. If we go in and take

everybody out, but we don't know who we looking for they can

always get a new crew and come back. The shit will never be

over." Suave said exactly what I was thinking.

"Damn, did yall friend go down there and cook an entire

meal?" Realizing Smalls never came back up, Suave gave me a

look and I knew what that meant.

"Purse dog, you and Blaze stay here with Face and light

anybody up that come in this mother fucker and it ain't us. Quick

come with me and Suave." They looked at us like we were crazy,

but they weren't like us. Even though they were street niggas, they

were a different kind. We knew when shit wasn't right and we

know Smalls. He looks for snacks or already cooked food. That nigga ain't about to cook shit his self. Easing down the stairs,

Suave stopped at the bottom, but didn't continue. He pointed at the

mirror on the wall and you could see Small's.

He was holding a baby and five niggas had they guns

pointed at him. He dropped his weapon and they grabbed the baby

from him and tied him to a chair. I knew Smalls and he kept quiet

because he didn't want them to know someone else was in the

house. This was the reason I always needed Suave with me, he was

the thinker. Had it been me, I would have went around the corner

blazing.

When Suave looked back at us, we raised our guns and me

and Quick knew we had to be fast and precise. On Suave's count,

we rounded the corner so fast they didn't have a chance to react.

Taking down four of them, neither of us hit the last one because he

was holding the baby.

"If you let the baby down, I won't kill you." Looking at his

crew, he decided to put the baby down. Once Quick had her, I

knocked his ass out. Untying Smalls, I noticed the fire on the stove

was on and it was a body in the kitchen.

"Nigga, you was actually about to cook a meal in their house?"

"Hell naw, when I made it down the stairs her bad ass was cutting the stove on. Before I could get to her a nigga grabbed her. he didn't see me so I laid his ass out. As soon as I picked her up, the others came in."

"Quick, go get your brothers. It's time to get some info out this mother fucker Lucifer's way." When Suave said that, my heart started racing. This was the shit I lived for. I was back.

CHAPTER 21- BABY FACE

When Quick came in and told us what went down, Blaze went crazy and I knew it wasn't gone be good for the nigga that was alive downstairs.

"Why they keep fucking with my daughter? You would think these nigga's beef was with me. I'm done playing bro. Yall can keep sitting around letting these niggas plot and just walk in our shit like they live here, but not me. I'm not sitting around waiting for them to hurt my child." Understanding where he was coming from, I knew we had to do something quick.

"I'm with Blaze on this shit. We not even safe in our own shit. They walking in and out her house at will. They want a war they got one."

"Calm down purse dog, you let a mother fucker walk all in our shit and beat your ass. How the fuck you gone stop a Cartel?" Laughing at Blaze comment, I knew Shadow ass wasn't gone find that shit funny.

"That nigga a contracted killer, how the hell was I gone win against that mother fucker?"

"You won't and that's why your ass need to fix your attitude. He was about to skin your ass until you were our color."

"At least you wouldn't look adopted no more." When Blaze said the last joke, Shadow walked out and we left out behind him.

"Fuck yall." By him being the youngest, we had to fuck with him. The shit will make him stronger. Blaze put Spark back in her room and closed the door.

"I don't even know how her lil ass got out of there anyway. She doing too much." Heading downstairs, we were all laughs and giggles until we rounded the corner and saw the set up Gangsta had. I hung around the nigga, I knew what he was about and saw it first hand. I don't think my brothers were ready for what was about to come.

Looking at all the knives he had on the table, I knew this was about to get ugly. The dude was knocked out cold and they were standing around waiting for him to wake up. I decided to help them out.

"Shadow." Nodding towards the guy, he walked over and knocked his eyes open.

"Damn purse dog, I'm glad I didn't give you the chance to swing first. That right hook nasty." Knowing G's rep, I knew that made Shadow feel good to hear that coming from an OG. Suave pulled up a chair and sat in front of the guy.

"I'm going to ask you some questions and depending on how you answer them will determine what happens next. Are we clear?" The guy nodded his head. "Good. Now who do you work for?" His eyes got big and he looked scared as hell. He was more afraid of the people he worked for. "I can see in your eyes that you fear your boss more and that is a very big mistake." Standing up, he moved his chair out the way.

"In this room we have a hit man, a fire starter, two niggas that can shoot you in seconds and you won't even see the gun, a nigga that could have been a heavy weight, and two of us that are quiet storms. Do you know what that mean?" the guy shook his head no and I felt bad for him.

"Gangsta, you're up." This nigga actually smiled as he walked over to the table and grabbed a knife. Smalls must be used to this shit as well because he stood there eating cookies and chips. G started carving the nigga's eye out and he screamed so loud I think he shook the house. When Gangsta got it out, Suave walked up again and I had no idea what was about to happen.

"Blaze you're up." I thought my brother was gone say hell naw you got me fucked up, but he walked up to G and took the eyeball. Standing in the man face, he set the eyeball on fire. When it fully caught fire, he dropped it to the floor and stepped on it. The sound of that shit smashing, turned my stomach. Shadow started throwing up and I knew he wouldn't be able to take much more of this. Blaze walked up to the bleeding eye socket and flicked his Bic. Holding the fire to it, the man finally screamed out.

"Okay I'll tell you whatever you want to know. Please stop." After a few more seconds, Blaze finally pulled back and walked off. Suave grabbed his chair again and sat back down.

"Who do you work for?"

"His name is Felipe. He is in charge of the entire Puerto Rico operation."

"How many estates do he have there?"

"Just the one."

"You said the Puerto Rico operation, what other countries do they have a faction in?"

"I don't know." Suave stood up again, and moved his chair.

"Gangsta, you're up." This time grabbing a different knife, he walked over to the man and grabbed his hand.

"I don't know, I promise I don't know." Suave wasn't moved and that let me know the man was lying. Suave can read anybody, this nigga gut was never wrong. Gangsta started peeling the skin from his fingers and worked his way up to his wrist.

"Oh God, please help me. Somebody help me. Oh God."

"Don't pray to God, pray to Lucifer." In one swift motion, he chopped off his hand.

"Blaze you're up." He walked over and flicked his Bic putting fire to the man's wrist. It wasn't until then, that I realized what Suave was doing. He was making Blaze burn him to stop the bleeding. He didn't want the man to die before he got all of the

information. Grabbing his chair again, he sat down.

"How many other factions are there and where are they?"

"Two more. Cuba and Columbia."

"Who is in charge of Felipe? Who is the head of all the

factions?" The man started crying, hell I wanted to cry for him. We

all knew what was about to happen next. Suave stood up and

moved the chair again.

"Gangsta, you're up." This time G grabbed a bottle and

walked over to him. Pouring it on the side of his face that wasn't

messed up, his shit started smoking and melting off. He was

pouring acid on him. Seeing the meat slide off his face, had me

ready to get the fuck out of there.

"It's a woman." Gangsta stopped pouring. Suave walked

over to him and sat down.

"Hold the fuck on, I ain't get my turn." Blaze was actually

pissed.

"What is her name?"

"Nobody knows, only Felipe. If you find Felipe he can take you to her." Stepping away from him, he spoke again.

"Shadow, Quick, Blaze, Face, Smalls, and G you're up." We all grabbed our guns and fired. He should be happy, there was no way I would have wanted to live life after that shit.

"Smalls, call the clean up crew. Hoover Gang, get ready we heading to Puerto Rico tomorrow."

"Yall niggas is sick." Smalls laughed as he grabbed his phone to make call. Looking at my brothers, we all had the same expression. We called the right niggas for the job.

CHAPTER 22- QUICK

Growing up, we all heard stories about Lucifer. Baby Face was the only one old enough to hang with them, but him and Blaze always connected. I think it was their I don't give a fuck attitude that drew them together. Even after the all the stories Face and Blaze told us, nothing could prepare me to see the shit up close and personal.

Not wanting to look like a bitch, it took everything in me not to throw the fuck up. When Shadow did it, I was glad to know I wasn't the only one bothered by the shit. At the end of the day, no matter how fucked up the shit was I'm glad they were there. If we couldn't get the job done with they ass, it was meant for The Hoover Gang to get laid down.

That thought alone scared the fuck out of me. When the clean up crew arrived, I walked outside to get some air. Heading down the driveway, I tried to clear my mind and couldn't. These niggas were coming at us hard over our father's debt. A nigga we didn't even fuck with. This shit needed to be over soon. My wife was about to have our baby and we couldn't be at war when that

happened. These niggas got us hiding out in our own shit like we

some bitch ass niggas.

"You good nigga?" Looking up, Blaze was standing there

looking at me crazy.

"Naw I'm not good. I'm not with this laying low shit.

When we go to Puerto Rico tomorrow, this shit has to end. We the

fucking Hoover Gang we don't duck no nigga and I ain't trying to

start that shit today."

"I'm ready too, these niggas keep coming for my baby and

I ain't having that shit. It's time to show them who the fuck they

dealing with."

"Damn nigga you ain't wash your hands after touching that

nigga eyeball? I always knew you were crazy, but I ain't know

your shit was twisted."

"You got me fucked up, nigga I almost fed that nigga my

breakfast. When Suave said I was up, I almost flicked my ass out

the fucking house and said fuck that Bic. Shit was nasty as hell, but

I couldn't let them show us up in our house. I ain't getting left off

bad and boujie."

"Shut your dumb ass up."

"No lie though, once I did it the shit gave me a rush like no

other. Yall think G is bad, but Suave is worse it just don't seem

that way because he so quiet."

"I can't imagine it being worse than that."

"Now yall done fucked up and let me like the shit. I'm

gone be cutting up body parts and setting it on fire. I wonder if

they can make a lighter with acid in it. Nigga yall eyebrows will

never come back if I had that shit." I'm glad he came out here and

had me laughing.

"Let's get back in here before they ass be done killed

Shadow." Agreeing, we turned around to walk in the house when

we heard the gun fire. Ducking down, we tried to run towards the

house.

"You strapped Blaze?" I was pissed that I left my shit in the

house.

"Fuck no, all I got is this mother fucking lighter. I'm about to throw this shit at a nigga."

"The fuck is that gone do?"

"Nothing, but at least I fought back. Your uglass ain't doing shit but dripping curl juice."

"We gotta make a run for it. We can't stay out here or we dead." Blaze counted down and we took off running. That nigga forgot about my ass and took off. As soon as I stood up, I got hit. My entire body shook and I hit the ground. The last thing I heard before my heart stopped was the gunfire getting closer. All I could do was pray that Blaze made it in the house safe. Closing my eyes, I knew it was over for me. My brothers would avenge me and take care of my seed. My work here was done.

CHAPTER 23- TANK

Getting off the plane, I was excited and scared at the same time. The stunt I was about to pull was going to have my marriage in jeopardy, but I didn't care. He would never go to war and I wasn't there to have his back. If he left me for that, then so be it. Looking over at Paradise, she had this look on her face that I never seen before. I knew that her and Gangsta killed together, but I never saw it with my own eyes. The look on her face scared me and in that moment I knew she was just like him. She looked soulless right now and if I didn't know her, I would fear for my life right now.

"Hey bitch, you good?"

"Yeah I'm straight. I'm just happy to be home." She down played that shit, but I could see it in her face that she was ready to kill some damn body. The bitch better wait until we drop these damn kids off. My friend Nik was here to pick us up and I was happy. A bitch was ready to go make sure my man was straight and I ain't have time to be waiting at a damn rental car counter. As soon as we got in the car, she started in.

"You know I don't mind keeping the kids cus Poo Poo will have somebody to play with, but Suave is going to kill you. Why do you insist on fighting him about this?"

"First off, you nick named your daughter a pile of shit? Secondly, I'm not fighting him he is the one making this hard. I'm not trying to be out here in these streets, but if that's where my man is then that's where I am."

"I'm just saying, you know how he is and you steady playing with fire."

"Look, I ain't trying to hear that shit. Where is the old Nik? We come from the same crew and now you done turned into a scary bitch."

"I got a family. You have to give shit up in order to make shit work."

"What the fuck has Smalls given up? You sounding like a weak bitch right now and anybody that know me knows I don't do that weak shit. You want to be a bitch, fine. Just leave that shit where you at. She choosing to ride for her man and you choosing to sit at home while your man out there at war. To each its own, but chill with all the fucking lectures and drive. Because if something happens to mine while you trying to preach, I'm coming back for your ass and I promise you not gone live to speak another fucking word. Now drive." I can tell it was some shit Nik wanted to say back to Paradise, but her scary ass knew better. This the bitch that created Lucifer, she better choose her battles wisely.

Pulling up to her house, she jumped out the car mad as hell. The shit was about to be awkward because Paradise still needed her to keep her bad ass daughter. How you gone curse out the bitch that's babysitting your kid? Laughing at the thought of Paradise having to play nice, I grabbed Deuce and headed inside.

"I appreciate you being concerned, but I got this sis. You just have to trust me." She hugged me and realized that Paradise hadn't come in.

"Girl go tell Paradise to bring me that damn baby. I'm not letting her go to war with her damn child in her arms."

"Oh I wasn't, this bad mother fucker took off down the damn street. I was bringing her in here and you was gone take her with a smile. Here." Passing her the baby, I looked at her in disbelief. Who in the fuck talks to somebody like that and make them watch they baby? Only Paradise. I mouthed thank you and we walked outside. Pulling my phone out, I was ready to call my cousins to see where they were. Before I could dial the number, they pulled up.

"What's up bitch." Laughing at Shay, me and Paradise walked up to the truck and got in.

"Shay and Bay Bay, this is Paradise. Paradise, these are my cousins and the other half of my crew. Did yall bring the heat."

"You know it. The bag is in the truck. You hoes ready?" Bay Bay was always in go mode.

"Let's ride. This is the address. I'm not sure if anything is going on right now, but when they leave to go to war we are going with them."

"I'm down, Gerald ass is getting on my nerves anyway. I wish he get the fuck on."

"I'm still in disbelief that you went back to that nigga."

"Don't worry about me, worry about this nigga Suave about to go upside your head." Everybody laughed and I see they all got jokes today. This was one ass whooping I was willing to take. Almost losing him broke me and I be damned if I go through the shit again.

When we pulled up to the house, I didn't know if this was where they were coming to take a mother fucker out or if this is where they were staying.

"Paradise, do you know who house this is?"

"Naw, he just said this was where they were going. Let's just sit here a minute and see what happens." Everyone agreed and we sat our ass and watched. After about ten minutes, a guy walked out.

"Damn that nigga fine. Sheit. Yall brought my ass to the right place." Bay Bay and Shay high fived and I silently agreed. When the next nigga walked out, my panties got wet.

"Okay, yall better not ever repeat this shit but I'll let them niggas run a train on me. The fuck. It's a house full of fine ass niggas. It better not be the niggas we gotta lay out because I swear

I'm not gone be able to do it. They too damn fine to be in

somebody damn grave."

"We here to help them. The last one to walk out is Blaze.

He used to be around G and them. Yall think he cute now, but the

nigga ignorant as fuck he will set your ass on fire in a minute."

"He can set this pussy on fire. Damn that nigga is

everything." Shay nasty ass was getting worked up.

"Hold up yall, you see them niggas right there?" I pointed

down the street and some niggas was coming fast as hell towards

the house, but they were bent down low. The fine niggas in the

drive way didn't see them coming.

"We don't know if G and them are here yet so we stay put."

I didn't agree with what Paradise was saying, so I kept my heat in

my hands ready to jump out at any minute. When the unknown

niggas started shooting in Blaze and them direction, we had to

wait. If we got out now, they would air our ass out. When they

walked towards the drive way, Blaze went running past and the

other nigga hit the ground. I was done waiting.

Jumping out the truck, I started blasting at they ass. Shay and Bay Bay followed suit and Paradise had no choice but to join us. In thirty seconds, we had laid all they asses out. When Blaze came out the door, he had his gun pointed at us.

"What the fuck. Paradise?"

"Yeah nigga and you welcome." We ran over to the other guy and he was laid out looking dead than a mother fucker.

"Macee, get your faking ass up. You was hit in the arm nigga." When I walked up, I saw the only hole on him was in his arm.

"Who the fuck are you and who the hell is Macee that faking ass nigga name is Quick."

"I'm Tank, Suave's wife and Quick ass was moving slow as fuck. Macee is this gay nigga in *Kb Cole book He Ain't Perfect, But He's Worth It* and his ass did the same dumb ass shit. Only thing Quick forgot to say was and scene."

"Girl, shut the fuck up. Nobody know who that nigga is. If he faking, why this nigga ain't got up yet?" This nigga Blaze was a rough one. I liked aggressive.

"I don't know, maybe he hit his head." Blaze leaned down and put a lighter to his face. As soon as he flicked that mother fucker, that nigga Quick shot up fast as hell.

"What happened." He looked around like he was lost.

"Nigga your ass fainted like a sissy in a book. Get up." Everybody started laughing and out of nowhere I was lifted in the air and slammed against the ground so hard a bitch couldn't breathe. For the first time since I met Suave, he looked soulless like Gangsta. His eyes had turned black and I saw no love there.

"Dammmmmmmnnnnn." It seemed like every nigga said it at the same damn time. The nigga never let my throat go.

"What the fuck did I tell you?" When I didn't respond, he pulled me up off the ground and slammed my ass again. "What the fuck did I tell you?"

"Nigga, she can't talk. You done knocked her vocal cord out her ass." He shot Blaze a look and the crazy nigga flicked his lighter. When he gave Suave a look like nigga try it, I wanted to laugh, but I couldn't. Finally, he released my neck and walked off.

He may leave me after this, but at least I knew he was safe. This was worth it to me and nobody else may never understand that shit.

"Tina. Hey Tina, you wanna borrow my lighter? You know Ike keep them good juices in his hair. I ain't never seen a nigga check a mother fucker that calm. You scared? You should be scared, hell I'm scared." Somebody better get this nigga. He fine as fuck, but this ain't the time to be joking. He play too damn much already.

Gangsta walked over to Paradise and kissed her. Why the fuck my man couldn't be happy to see me. Sitting up, I wanted to yell this was some bullshit, but I think my ass was still in my back.

"Sis you good?" Rolling my eyes at G, I stood up and went to go find my man.

"You got some leaves in your hair." This nigga was aggy as hell.

"Fuck you." Walking in the house, I prayed my husband wasn't done with me.

CHAPTER 24- SUAVE

When we heard the gun shots, we all had to take cover.

None of us had our weapons on us and that was a bad move on our

part. Baby Face made his way through the gun fire up the stairs to

make sure the baby was good. As weak as they thought Shadow

was, that nigga play no games. Trying to get outside to his

brothers, I had to hold him down until the gun fire ceased. He was

in protect mode, but what he was doing wasn't smart. All we could

do was pray that Quick and Blaze was straight.

The shooting stopped for a brief second and then started

back up. Once it completely stopped, we waited a minute before

we moved just in case they were trying to trap us. Finally easing

off the floor, Smalls made his way to the window and started

laughing. Me and Shadow looked at him like he was crazy.

"You niggas in here on the floor hiding and shit, but you

got reinforcement out here."

"Fuck you talking about?"

"All imma say is them niggas dead as shit out there. You think they will care if I grab some more snacks?"

"Nigga all your ass care about is eating. Who the fuck out there?"

"Come see for yourself." When I got to the window and saw Tank and her crew with guns drawn and making sure they were all dead, I saw red. This mother fucker deliberately said fuck me. Punching the wall, I tried to calm down. Looking back out the window, I saw her all he he ha ha with Blaze and that shit pissed me off. Not because I was jealous, but the fact that she thought the shit was sweet.

"G, you told Paradise where we were going?"

"Yeah, just in case our ass didn't come home she knew where to start looking. Why what happened." This nigga was lying and you would think he would know not to lie to me after all these years.

"Quit lying nigga, I'll deal with you later. Right now I'm about to beat the jet lag out her ass." Walking out the door, I was trying to tell myself to calm down, but the more she talked and laughed the madder I got. She was so deep in her conversation she didn't even see me walking up on her. Grabbing her by her neck, I lifted her ass in the air and tried to take her ass through the concrete. When she wouldn't answer me, I wanted to knock her ass out, but the fear in her eyes stopped me. I'm not the type of nigga that hit on females, but I swear she the only one that ever made me come close.

She was always pushing her limit and I didn't like the way she made me stoop to this level. Not wanting to kill her I walked off. Seeing all the bodies laid out, I smiled on the inside. Not wanting my chick in these streets had nothing to do with me not wanting her to get hurt, but she ain't no damn nigga and I wanted her to be a wife and a mother to my child.

Every time I tried to be mad at her for doing shit like this, I ended up proud or happy as fuck. Her hard head ass be putting in work and you can't be mad at that. I'm sure Blaze and Quick happy as hell because they saved their lives, but I wanted to be mad. Knowing we all could possibly be dead, I decided to give her another pass. I won't let her know that I was happy as fuck they showed up when they did, but I was. Reaching the kitchen, Smalls ass was in there making a sandwich.

"Nigga call the clean up crew back and tell they ass to come quick. These niggas outside and we don't want them to be out there long. Even though nobody lives on his block, we don't want a mother fucker to end up driving pass. Heading outside, I stood in the yard and tried to collect my thoughts. The streets have a way of sucking a nigga back in. This was the most excitement I had in a minute and I didn't want to admit that I was loving this shit.

My family was more important than this shit, but the streets ran through my blood. Once this was over, it was back to my life as a retired King Pin. While I was here, I would enjoy this shit.

"Kendyl, can I talk to you please?" Turning around, Tank was standing there with tears in her eyes. Everything about her turned me on and knowing she just put in work had my dick hard. Walking up to her fast, she closed her eyes and flinched not knowing what I was about to do. Grabbing her by her neck, I lifted her off her feet all the way in the air and slammed her against the wall. Using my free hand, I snatched her leggings down and started sucking on her clit. My wife never wore panties and that always gave a nigga easy access. When she realized what I was doing, she wrapped her legs around my neck and I continued to suck the soul out her ass.

She couldn't take the assault I was putting on her pussy and started shaking, sticking my tongue inside her I caught all her nut and went right back to her clit. She tried to grab my head and I slammed her back against the wall. Never taking my hand from around her neck, I applied just enough pressure.

Cumming a second time, I knew she was ready for the dick. Dropping my jogging pants down, I slammed her down on my dick without warning or prepping her. Using her neck as grip, I brought her up and down on my dick hard as hell. Knowing I didn't want to hit her, I beat her pussy up instead. Every time she tried to moan or scream out, I squeezed harder and slammed her against the wall.

She was gone take this dick and shut the fuck up. Feeling my nut rising, I slid her off my dick and pushed her down to her knees. Pushing my dick in her mouth, she tried to take all of me in slow. Grabbing her by her head, I fucked her face until I was cumming down her throat.

"Fuuuuckkk." Knowing I was weak, she started going crazy on my dick making sure she got every last drop. When my knees started shaking, I knew I couldn't take no more. Pulling her head back, she stood up and pulled her clothes up.

"Damn Tina, you took that ass whooping like a G. Hey Suave I fucks with you and all, but don't be fucking in my yard nutting on my walls and shit. I started to burn your ass hairs off. Nigga why you got hair back there any damn way? You think you in Nutbush city for real huh?" This nigga Blaze didn't give a fuck what he said out his mouth.

"Nigga get the fuck on before I think you saw my girl naked and if I think that shit, I'm not gone let you live to tell it."

"Chill out my nigga, I ain't seen shit. Her shit look in tact tho my wife shit looser than a jherri curl." He walked off before I could slap the shit out his ass. This nigga play too much. After fixing ourselves up, we walked back in the house and everybody was in the kitchen.

"This house not safe and I'm not staying here waiting on these niggas to keep coming back so what's the plan."

"Our family at the main house, we can all go there it's big enough for everybody. Tomorrow we leave for Puerto Rico as planned. If most of they niggas here, it should be easy to penetrate they shit." Baby Face made a point and I agreed.

"Paradise already took care of my bullet wound so I'm good to go. We need to get the fuck up out of this mother fucker right now. A nigga thought he was gone."

"How Sway? You got shot in the arm and passed out like a ran through sissy." Everybody laughed at Blaze and got ready to head out.

"Wait, everybody staying at the main house? We never bring people to the main house."

"Damn purse dog, I thought we got pass that shit. Nigga your ass will sleep on the porch before me."

"Shut the fuck up damn, I was talking about them." We looked over and he was talking about Shay and Bay Bay.

"Damn purse nigga toughening up. I like that lil nigga, but don't bark if you not gone bite and they cool they with us." Gangsta liked fucking with Shadow and it was funny to see them going back and forth.

"Then it's settled, let's roll." I think G likes Shadow, he got a lot of heart to be that young.

"Hey can I have one of these Lunchables?" Everybody looked at Smalls and laughed.

"Damn nigga, you gone owe us some money in a minute. Your hungry ass better go eat some pussy or something." Baby Face was joking, but I swear Smalls will eat all your shit. We headed out the house and drove over to the main house.

CHAPTER 25- BABY FACE

Juicy picked a helluva time to leave, these chicks that came with Suave's wife was fine as fuck and I was ready to put Tsunami in somebody life. Getting ready to head to the main house, I shook my head at all the shit going on, it was gone be hell being under the same roof. Add all of us and my mama to the mix, this was a recipe for disaster. When I headed to my Hummer, one of the fine chicks walked over with me.

"Can I ride with you?" Knowing this was not a good idea, I let my dick answer for me.

"Yeah." Trying my best not to look thirsty, I played the shit off cool and just jumped in. About to turn up my radio, to avoid any conversation but she deadened that shit.

"What's your name?"

"Baby Face and yours?"

"I'm Shay and I'm Tank's cousin. Where your girl at?" Even though Juicy left and I wanted to say I ain't have a girl, I knew I should keep this situation under wraps. This shit could get complicated and a nigga didn't need that shit.

"I'm married and we on a break."

"Can you fuck another chick on this break?" Tsunami damn near jumped out my pants when she said that shit. My ass wanted to scream fuck yeah, but I tried my best to keep this shit cool.

"We never talked about that. I see you a live one huh? Straight to the fucking point. You trying to fuck Shay?" Why the fuck did I ask that. She slid her hand in her pants and started fingering herself. Her shit was gushy as fuck and I damn near crashed trying to look. When she slid her hand out and tried to stick it in my mouth, I straightened up quick as fuck.

"Hold on ma, I don't eat random pussy. You fine as fuck, but I ain't going there." Seeing the disappointment on her face, I tried to redirect it. My ass wanted to see the rest of the show. "Let me see how you suck it. This dick big as fuck and I need to know if I'm gone be wasting my time." Sliding her fingers in her mouth, I almost leaned over and sucked them mother fuckers with her. She was doing that shit so sexy, it took everything in me not to fuck her

right now. Needed to slow this shit down, I tried to talk with her.

"Why your fine ass ain't got a nigga?"

"Who said I didn't?"

"My bad, I assumed you didn't because your ass in here

ready to fuck and you don't know me like that."

"He fucking up right now and I need some dick. Are we

really gone sit here and talk about my nigga when you got all this

good pussy right here?"

"I would talk about my dick, but man that shit would be a

long story." She laughed as I quoted Lil Wayne.

"Let me see."

"Let you see what? My dick?" When she nodded her head,

I could see it was gone be hard to turn her ass down.

"It ain't enough room in this mother fucker to pull this

bitch out." Out of nowhere, she straightened up and her demeanor

changed. Thinking she must have an attitude, I turned the music up

the shit was for the best anyway. When we pulled up to the house,

I barely parked the mother fucker before she jumped her lil ass out.

Used to feisty chicks, the shit didn't bother me. Everybody else

pulled up and Gangsta got out holding Spark. If I didn't know he

had a baby, I could never picture him with a child. This nigga

looked like he ate children and shit. Heading in the house,

everybody was already in the front like they knew we were

coming.

Drea saw Spark and took off running towards Gangsta.

"You can slip on his dick if you want to I'll have your

pussy looking like burnt Italian beef. Back your ass up. No

disrespect to you Gangsta, but my wife like to bust it open. That

pussy like an 89 Cutlass, mother fucker got some mileage." Blaze

was never gone let Drea live that shit down.

"Shut up Blaze, I was going to get Spark." Reaching for the

baby, she had tears in her eyes as she kissed her a million times.

"I'm just saying, you was running kind of fast in those

socks your ass might have slipped." We all shook our head at the

nigga and walked all the way in. Zavi and Ash ran to Quick, while

Shadow picked Kimmie's big ass up in the air and hugged her.

Everybody had somebody welcoming them back but me and the shit pissed me off.

"Yall got me fucked up leaving me with these worrying ass bitches. Yall need to toughen they ass up. Every time I tried to get this thang ate one of them was knocking on the door trying to talk and shit. A bitch ain't got no dick since yall ass been gone." Gangsta, Suave and they crew looked in horror as my mama showed her ass.

"Is this ma dukes? Nigga I'm criiinnee." Smalls was dying laughing and my mama finally noticed them.

"Devon you can go home now. They done brought mama a house full of young dick. Damn yall fine, which one of yall wanna sample this tiger pussy." Before I could warn her, Paradise damn near made my mama wig fly off she ran up on her so fast.

"That one there is mine, keep your teeth in your mouth and stay away from him." I knew Paradise was crazy, but she didn't know my mama was just as loony.

"Hold on Devon don't leave yet, hold my wig. This mother fucker got me fucked up. Sons I'm about to whoop her ass, but make sure you break it up in five minutes. After that, a hoe won't

be able to breathe and yall better not let her beat yall mama ass.

Shadow go get me some water and have it on standby. Now you,

what you wanna do lil bitch cause you got me fucked up. If I

wanna suck his dick, I'm gone suck the skin off that mother

fucker." She actually handed her wig to Devon and his slow ass

stood there and held it.

"Ma, go sit your old ass down somewhere. Nobody fucking

that old ass wolf pussy. You do the most." She looked at Quick

like she wanted to beat his ass.

"Don't worry about it bitch, I know somebody that like it."

Laughing, I prayed the tension would die down. Paradise was still

staring my mama down, but I would give her a fade so fast if she

touched my mama.

"Everybody, this is Gangsta aka Lucifer and his wife

Paradise, Suave and his wife Tank, Shay, Bay Bay, and Smalls. Ma

Smalls girl ain't here so he up for grabs." Blaze wasn't shit for

throwing Smalls under the bus like that.

"Lucifer? Oh hell no, I heard all the stories. You won't get this tiger. Mother fucker might pour acid on my shit and my hair long, acid gone catch hold of that shit and burn this pussy up. Girl you can pick your face up and stop mugging I don't want his ass. Nigga might kill my poor tiger dead. The mother fucker already old. Come on Devon, give me my shit and let me show you this new trick I saw on Porn Hub." She grabbed her wig and threw it on her head and was gone.

"Nigga that's a damn shame. If Paradise leave your ass you ain't never gone be able to get no pussy." Laughing at Smalls, everybody started to relax and started mingling. On my way to the kitchen, I overheard Shay talking to her sister.

"Girl yeah, he too fine to have a lil ass dick."

"He showed it to you?"

"Nope, as soon as I asked he bitched up and wouldn't let me see. That mean that mother fucker gotta be small." Now, I could have let her have that shit because I knew my dick size, but I wanted to shut her the fuck up. Turning around, I walked over to them and grabbed her by the arm. I damn near dragged her ass up the stairs.

"What the fuck you doing? Let me go." Not responding, I drug her all the way to my room. Pushing her down to the floor, I didn't even let her get on the bed.

"Take that shit off."

"Nigga please, I don't give away sympathy pussy. I'm sorry if I bruised your ego, but you not hitting this."

"I'm not gone ask you again." When she looked into my eyes, she slid her pants off and laid there looking ready. She was gone get the dick, but not yet. "Play with that pussy." Needing her to get it ready, I was gone fuck but I wasn't eating no pussy to get it wet. She wanted to talk all that shit, I should have went in her shit before it got wet but a nigga didn't want a murder charge.

Hearing that mother fucker talking to me, I was ready to shut her the fuck up. Walking over to her, she spread her legs like she thought it was time for that. Grabbing her by her hair, I pulled her up to her knees.

"Damn nigga that hurt." Dropping my pants, I freed Tsunami and her eyes damn near fell out her head. My dick was damn near bigger than her body and she talking shit. Without warning, I pushed my dick in her mouth and made her head go all the way to my balls. Gagging out of control, spit flew everywhere. Go figures, talk all that shit and can't even suck this big mother fucker. Guiding her head up and down my dick slowly, I let her throat relax before I slammed it all the way in again. Her eyes got watery and I eased up. Moving it slowly, she tried to go crazy and I slammed it back down again.

She was gone think about shit the next time she tried to talk about a nigga. Realizing she wasn't gone be able to take much more of Tsunami being in her throat, I pulled out and walked to the dresser and grabbed a condom. Strapping up, I walked over to her and picked her up. Putting her on the bed, I made her do a head stand. By her being so short, it wouldn't have worked with her on the floor. Hands on the mattress, face down and ass up I slid my dick in her and she immediately screamed out.

"Fuck, wait your shit too big."

"Naw, you said my dick was little and now you gone take this shit. Grabbing her by her waist, I rocked her back and forth on this mother fucker until I got it all in. That's the reason I picked this position because she couldn't do shit but take all of it. She kept trying to run, but I started slamming this dick all in her pussy. My ass was so deep I think I felt her heart beat. Slapping her ass so hard, my hand print was left on that yellow mother fucker.

"Don't get quiet now." Slapping her ass again, she screamed.

"Fuck, I'm sorry. Fuck this shit so big." She tried to get away again, but I had her ass on lock.

"Take this dick. Quit running." Tired of fighting with her ass, I grabbed her legs and put them around my waist. Grabbing her hips, I slammed her on this dick until I felt my nut rising. Filling the condom with my nut, my body shook and I laid on top of her. After I caught my breath, I rolled over and she was still unable to move.

"Go get your bag so you can take a shower. You staying in here with me tonight, I'm gone fuck you until you able to take it." She groaned and got up and did what I asked.

When she came back up, we showered together and headed downstairs with everybody else. Her sister saw how she was walking and tried to whisper in her ear.

"I'm guessing his dick wasn't little, bitch he fucked you bowleg." Laughing, I walked over to the fellas to talk shit.

"Hey quick question, why yall got this big ass picture of Blaze in here like this nigga dead or something?" Smalls was looking confused and I tried to explain it to him.

"The nigga died and we got it done." Before I could finish explaining what happened, Smalls pulled his gun out and pointed it at Blaze.

"Yall telling me this nigga a ghost? Suave yall know I don't play that ghost shit. Why the fuck yall ain't tell me this nigga was dead? Nigga I swear to God if you come through my walls tonight I'm gone air your ass out." Everybody looked at him like he was crazy and fell out laughing.

"Nigga what the fuck are you talking about? I fake died, but they didn't know it when they got this pic." Slowly putting his gun away, he reached out and touched Blaze.

"Aww okay you did that shit Suave did. Yall niggas gone quit playing with me with the dead. That shit creeps me the fuck out." He relaxed some, but he still never took his eyes off Blaze. I couldn't do shit but laugh, these niggas was crazy as fuck and I was gone be pissed when they left. We all needed this last hoorah.

CHAPTER 26- GANGSTA

Paradise was ready to kill they mama, but I wasn't gone let that shit go down like that. These my niggas and that's their OG, Paradise was acting like I would really fuck her old ass. My baby still got jealous and I thought the shit was cute. It's been a long time since she felt intimidated.

From their mama talking shit and my niggas cutting up, a nigga barely wanted to go back home. A nigga was already missing the kill, but this shit was life. We were having a fucking ball and I hated that tomorrow, it was a chance that one of us may not come back. It's always a risk we take when we go to war. That shit wasn't gone be easy to take us down, but it was always a possibility. Deep in my own thoughts, I didn't see purse dog wife walk up on me.

"They over there telling stories about you and I'm intrigued. How the hell did you turn into the devil?" She looked like she was actually excited, but I wasn't a friendly nigga. Since I already fucked her nigga up, I decided to be nice.

"The streets named me Lucifer. They said when you look in my eyes you didn't see shit, but death. When I killed people felt only a nigga with no soul could do the shit I did. Suave started it and it kind of stuck."

"I get that, but what did you do that made them say that? Murder is murder right?" Damn this girl talk a lot. She asking a million questions and she so into it her ass don't even know she in danger. Paradise was burning a hole through her head.

"Because me and my girl cut my parents up and made a game out of it."

"Wait what?" The excitement was replaced by disgust and it took everything in me not to laugh in her face.

"Who in the hell would do something like that?"

"Lucifer." Staring at her my eyes went cold. I didn't like the judgment in her eyes. "Would you like to meet him?"

"What the fuck is that supposed to mean? Are you threatening me?" She was getting loud and starting to piss me off.

"I don't throw threats, but I can tell you this you close to bringing him out."

"I'm not sure who the fuck you're used to dealing with, but." That's all she got out before I had her off her feet in the air by her neck. She was pushing my buttons and I didn't like that shit.

"You got one more time and your ass gone regret ever meeting me." Out of nowhere, my head snapped back and I dropped her big ass. This nigga Shadow had socked the shit out my ass. Paradise ran up on Kimmie and they started rumbling. Turning towards Shadow, I was about to react when Blaze went over to Paradise and lit her ear on fire. Who in the fuck burns an ear? The house was about to go crazy and I wasn't for the dumb shit.

"ENOUGH." Everybody stopped and looked at me like they were scared. The entire house was ready to meet Lucifer. Turning to Shadow, I licked the blood from my mouth. The nigga stood his ground and I walked up on him. You could hear a pin drop in that bitch.

"It's about time purse dog. Who knew all I had to do was go at your girl to bring the beast out your ass. Make sure you have that mother fucking monster in your ass tomorrow." Walking towards the fellas, I turned back around.

"Oh and purse dog, if you ever hit me like that again, I'll cut your hand off and feed it to your wife."

"Nigga shut your sick ass up and go check on your wife. I don't think her ass can hear you." Laughing at Blaze, I wanted to slap his ass. This nigga played so much, he lucky I fucked with his ass tough.

"Blaze I swear your ass ain't shit. Why would you burn me nigga?"

"Sis I been looking at that mother fucker all day. Who the fuck got pretty ears, a nigga been waiting to get them mother fuckers." Everybody laughed and went back to mingling. Shadow didn't know it, but I was proud of him. His brothers were a different kind of monster, but he was still reserved. I been trying to get that beast out of him all day. First time I looked in his eyes, I saw potential. In another day and time, I would make him my protégé. He had it in him to be worse than all of us, a mother fucker just needed to bring it out of him.

"You gone have my baby brother thinking you don't like him." Baby Face knew me and he knew I took a liking to purse dog.

"That's because he don't know me."

"Aight yall we out, I'm about to go fuck my girl before she get horny and you niggas run a train on her ass." Laughing at Blaze, him and his family headed upstairs and we all sat around talking shit and having a good time. This was the life and I prayed tomorrow we all made it out.

After about an hour of us all sitting around kicking it, Paradise got up and went upstairs. Knowing I needed to get in them guts, I thought it was best that everybody laid it down. We had a long day ahead of us.

"Aight yall, go be with your families and get some rest, on tomorrow we go to war. See yall in the a.m." Everybody finished up and headed upstairs. When I got in the room, Paradise came in five minutes after me. I was about to ask her what the hell was she doing, but I just wanted some pussy and sleep. Taking my clothes off, I motioned for her to come over to me.

"Come suck this dick." Her eyes lit up and I knew this was about to be a good nut.

****

The next morning, we were all downstairs waiting on Blaze to grace us with his presence so we could go handle business. Everybody was just sitting around talking when Blaze came running down the stairs screaming.

"Who the fuck did it? Which one of you mother fuckers want to play these games. I'm about that fire life and one of you mother fuckers just kicked off a war." We all looked up at him and this nigga had one eyebrow and half of his mustache was gone. We laughed so fucking hard, my side was killing me. "This shit ain't funny, my shit just grew back."

"At least you not blank son. Now we can call you half assed." They mama was hell and she kept my ass laughing. When everybody kept laughing, but nobody would say anything, he started snapping.

"Okay. Alright. I'm taking eyebrows off all you bitches. You think you can do this shit to me? You mother fuckers will be walking around hairless in Pelican Bay when I get finished with you. Shoe program nigga. Twenty three hour lockdown. I'm the fucking man up in this piece." When we realized this nigga was doing his version of Denzel Washington in Training Day, it wasn't a dry eye in the room we were laughing so hard.

"I run shit here, you just live here. You better walk away. I'm gone burn this mother fucker down. King Kong ain't got shit on me. I'm winning anyway. I can't lose. I'm fine as fuck and that eyebrow ain't gone make me." This nigga was doing the hand movements, laughs and all. I was fucking done. I don't think I laughed that hard in my life.

"Nigga shut up and go let that girl go draw you an eyebrow on so yall can hurry up and go handle this shit. I'm ready to go home and fuck in my own bed. I'm in a house full of Jeffry Dahmers, Wayne Gacy's, and OJ Simpsons and shit. Too many sick mother fuckers in here for me, my damn tiger won't get wet because I'm too nervous. Mother fucker might come in and try to take my shit." Debra ass was hell.

"Ma don't nobody want that dry ass pussy. Shit probably sound like corduroy pants rubbing together. Get yo life. You can call me half assed, but I'm gone call your ass Sandman." Blaze walked off to go get his brows done.

"I hate you mother fuckers, who raised yall ass?" We all looked at Debra and laughed.

Blaze finally came downstairs with his new brows and shit.

"Nigga you look like an Instagram Model." Smalls ass stayed trying to go in on a nigga. We grabbed our weapons and got ready to head to this plane.

"We don't have to go to Puerto Rico yall." Looking over at Shadow, I got disappointed.

"Damn purse dog, I thought you found your back bone last night."

"Back deez nuts. We don't have to go to Puerto Rico because they are here. The entire house is surrounded." Jumping from joke mode, we all went into killer mode instantly. Easing to the windows, we looked out and they definitely had us surrounded.

"Drea, go get all the kids, mama, and the pastor and take them in the basement. Don't bring yall ass out until I come get you." The funny Blaze was gone and we got ready to go to war. Even the girls were in go mode.

"We gone have to split up in order to cover the entire grounds. The girls can't be by themselves so we mix it up. Gangsta, Blaze, me and Smalls will take the front. Shadow, Paradise, and Shay yall take the East. Tank, Quick, Bay Bay and Suave yall take the back. We will all work our way to the West. Everybody good?"

"Suave go with Shadow, Quick got the back on lock and now we good." Everybody nodded and went to their perspective place. Within seconds, all you heard was gun fire. We were dropping the niggas in the front like flies and it felt good to be back. Wherever I heard the wind blow, I was letting my shit rip. Turning to get a nigga that was on the roof, I didn't see a nigga creep up on me. My instincts kicked in and I felt him behind me, by the time I turned, it was too late. Paradise ran in front of me and he lit her up. Her body was jerking left and right. I went crazy and

I didn't stop shooting until every gun of mine was empty. His face was gone and I kept shooting. I was so pissed, I didn't even realize all the other gun fire had stopped.

"Baby bro, he dead. Let's get Paradise to the hospital." I was so stuck looking at the holes in her body, I broke down. "Come on baby bro, we have to go. If we want to save her, we have to leave now." Picking her up, I cradled her and carried her to the car.

"Blaze and Shadow come with us, the rest of yall stay here. Smalls call the clean up crew. I'll keep yall updated." Suave started barking orders, but I didn't care about shit but my wife. Why the fuck would she jump in front of me like that. If anybody deserved to die, it was me. A nigga did so much in his life it was only right I went to meet the real Lucifer. Seeing her body jerk like that, man I can't get that image out my head.

As soon as we got to the hospital, they took her in the back and we were left waiting. If I lost my wife, the entire world was gone bleed until I found the head of that Cartel. Mother fuckers didn't want to feel my wrath, but they were about to. She was the good part of me. In that moment, I understood why she wanted us

out this life. This was the part I didn't miss. When the smoke

cleared, we had to hope everybody was left standing. My brother

knew what I was going through because he was in this same place

with Tank. Sitting down beside me, he didn't say anything, but him

being here meant a lot. She had to make it.

****

After waiting five hours, they finally came back and told us

they were able to remove all the bullets, but one. It was too risky

right now, but she was stable. They had her sedated, but they let us

back to see her. We were standing in the room and I could hear

heels coming down the hall. For some reason, the sound was

drawing me to it. Looking at the door, a woman walked in. She

was older and looked like she was Puerto Rican or some shit.

"Hello Gangsta and Suave. So I get the pleasure of seeing

you again."

"Who the fuck are you?" This wasn't the time for games.

"Mary Garzon, head of the Garzon Cartel." She looked at

me and waited for me to put it together. This was Paradise's mother. Before I could extend my hand to her and update her on Paradise, she started talking again.

"I take it that you now know who I am. When you killed my husband and all of his men, that left me in charge. You know, the head bitch in charge." She was walking around the room like she owned it and we hung on to every word trying to see where she was going with this convo.

"My mama always said women were smarter than men and I proved her right. Using the money I had and my smarts, I was able to expand the Cartel and have different factions but we will get back to that.

I see only half of the Hoover Gang is in attendance, I hope everyone is okay." She smirked and now I was really trying to figure out what this bitch was on. "Blaze and Shadow, you can count out ten million dollars in your sleep why wouldn't you just pay the money?"

"Wait, you're the one that Rico owed the money to? I'm confused." Blaze wasn't catching on, but I understood it clear.

"Blaze, it seems like we have a common enemy. Paradise mom is the same person your dad owed and the person we have been looking for. She is the head of the faction in Puerto Rico. What I want to know is, did you know that Paradise was there when you sent your men?" Now this was the answer I wanted to know and I was glad Suave asked it.

"Of course, I was there at Blaze house when she took out half of my men. It was interesting that one crew I been looking for happened to come help the other crew I was now at war with. I'm able to kill two birds with one stone. You think you were going to use this lil bitch of mine to kill my husband and get away with it? Didn't she teach your dumb ass anything." Before I knew it, I had my hand around her neck slamming her head against the wall.

"G, let her go. You can't do this here or you're going to jail. Gangsta, listen to your big bro let her go." Squeezing one last time, I let her down and she laughed.

"In due time gutter rat, we will meet again." She tried to turn and walk away, but Blaze ran up on her before she made it out the door. He flicked that Bic and her hair caught fire fast as hell.

She was standing there screaming and trying to put it out, when this nigga drop kicked her in the ass. Her and that flaming hair went flying into the hallway. I prayed the bitch hit her head and died. Walking to the door, I looked out and didn't see any men with her. The nurses grabbed her and I walked back in Paradise's room.

"We may have taken out most of her crew. She is going to go home to Puerto Rico or Columbia and regroup. I'll have somebody follow her and we gone take the war to her old ass. This shit ain't over." This bitch had to go.

CHAPTER 27- SHADOW

Looking at Gangsta right now, I knew shit was about to go all bad. When Paradise mother was talking to us, he stared at her intently. The minute she admitted to shooting his girl, his eyes went cold. I had never witnessed someone cut their emotions that fast. Even now, he is just standing here zoned out. Looking in his eyes, you see nothing. Realizing now why G was fucking with me, I could actually feel sympathy for him.

Mother fuckers always looked at me as the weak link because I was the baby. Instead of him making fun of me and just teasing me about it, he decided to help me. Now I would have preferred for him to let me know what the fuck he was doing, but I get it. Watching him in action back at Blaze house, I didn't want to be in the room. Seeing my brothers stand there and not flinch showed me it was a lot I needed to learn.

People feared them off their name alone, mother fuckers only feared me because of my last name. I wanted the same respect that they had. Growing up, everybody heard stories about Suave and Gangsta. If I had known that's who was at the fucking door, I would have just let the nigga in. A nigga needed his tongue to eat pussy and that nigga G known for snatching parts off a mother fucker. That demon that they possess, I don't have it. Even Blaze have that same sick way about him. Being around them, I never noticed how I didn't equal up to them because we did everything together.

It took for Gangsta to come and show me my weakness. The good thing was, I'm only twenty two. My ass can learn and adapt. The only problem with that is, now that I wanted to learn to be that ruthless ass nigga we were out of the game. Deep in my own thoughts, so many insecurities I didn't know I had surfaced. My weakness was the same reason the women in my life always walked over me. Kimmie was different and I couldn't allow him to hurt her. That's how I know she was my soul mate. If it had been Shirree ass issa funeral. There was no way I would have got in that shit and risked that nigga cutting my hand off.

Now appreciative of the legends that was standing before me, I could work on that shit. No matter what, Shadow wasn't gone be that young weak nigga no more. It was time for me to step out of my brother's shadow and man the fuck up. Walking over to G, I didn't know what to say. Hell, it didn't even seem like the nigga was here. Ain't no telling who this nigga was standing in the room, he liable to kill all our ass. Since I was on my grown man shit now, I threw caution to the wind and spoke up.

"I'm sorry you going through this and I just wanted you to know we here. Whatever you need us to do, we got your back." When that nigga turned to face me, his eyes scared me so bad a silent fart seeped out. My ass was praying it didn't stank because the way he was looking, he might kill my ass for it. He turned his head back towards Paradise and didn't address what I said at all. Looking at Blaze, he nodded his head in approval. It was fucked up because his girl was in this position over our bullshit.

As if Suave could hear what I was thinking, he spoke up.

"A couple of years ago, we were in this same position. He doesn't blame you. Our loyalty is strong and we knew the risks when we came back. He's blaming his self for letting her come. I'm not going to tell you it's going to be okay, but know that in this moment you are dealing with the worse side of him. They just unleashed something he fought so hard to bury. It's not going to be pretty and he won't stop until they are all dead. We need you to be ready and trained to go. It can go from worse to bad and we can lose more people along the way, but no matter what we don't stop until it's done."

"Bro you know we got you. I stay ready and we feel the same way. When do we leave?"

"Tomorrow, we will go while she is still weak from losing so many men."

"No. We wait for Paradise. No matter how I feel, that is her mother. I didn't kill her father and I won't kill her mother. The only way we kill that bitch is if she refuses to do it." Gangsta finally spoke.

"Do you think she will do it?" If it was me, there is no way I could kill my mom. Blaze ass would have no problems doing it though.

"She the one that created Lucifer. She trained me." Nothing else needed to be said. That just told me that her ass just as crazy as him or maybe worse since she made him the way he is. Looking

at her laying in the bed, I'm glad she made it. Now she needed to

get her ass up so we can finish what they started.

****

Walking into the house, we were exhausted. G refused to

leave until Paradise opened her eyes. Unfortunately for us, that shit

took two days. We couldn't leave him there because we didn't

know if that bitch would return and try to finish off Paradise.

Gangsta said he was having her followed and I didn't understand

why he didn't just have her killed. The nigga told me where was

the fun in that. He was certified crazy.

Kimmie walked up to me crying and everybody looked at

us with sadness in their eyes.

"She is okay. We came to take a shower and change

clothes. We will do shifts and take turns staying with Gangsta until

she gets out of there. No one is to be left alone. If I'm at the

hospital Quick you are to stay here. We need precise shooters at

both locations at all times. Tank if any of the women have to go anywhere, you and Face will make sure you are with them. Smalls, can you get your crew to stand guard outside?"

"I'll put them lil niggas out there. We can take turns guarding the back."

"How long do we have to do this for?" Drea was looking worried.

"Until Paradise comes home. When she does, we head to Columbia. Everybody stay on point. No more playing and no bullshitting around. When all this is over, I'm going to figure out which one of yall did this shit to my eyebrow and its war. My shit was just growing back." That was the first time we laughed in a couple of days. Kimmie pulled me to the side and held me.

"Baby, I'm so scared. This is some real life movie shit. I just want to go home."

"This is your home for now. If you gone be married to me, then you have to be okay with shit like this. We gone end it as soon as possible. I promise." I prayed nobody else got hurt.

CHAPTER 28- BLAZE

Standing there listening to Paradise's mother pissed me off. Who the fuck shoots their own fucking child and stand there and brag about it. By the time she turned to walk out the door, I had never wanted to burn somebody so bad in my life. I couldn't imagine what G was feeling right then, but I knew when we got to Columbia it was gone be all bad. His eyes were so empty the nigga was giving me goose bumps. A nigga had never been happier to see a mother fucker open their eyes. She scanned the room looking for G and as soon as her eyes landed on his, she started crying.

He climbed in the bed with her and that shit made me feel some type of way. In a sense, it had me realizing what my family was going through when I fake died.

"Why the fuck would you jump in front of me? Don't ever do that shit again."

"I'll do that shit a million times my nigga. Life without you in it ain't living." He kissed her and the shit was so sweet it made me want to go home and hold my wife. We didn't know how this shit was gone end, or if all of us would make it out. No matter what, we had to finish this shit.

"I have something to tell you. The person that we are here to kill is your mom. She is the head of the Cartel and she tried to take you out." When he said that, she sat up and looked him in the eyes. The bitch ain't even wince from the pain.

"How do you know that?"

"She came here and bragged about it." The room got silent and I wondered what she was thinking.

"Sis, you know what needs to happen. G wants to give you the respect of doing it yourself, are you okay with that." We all looked at her and in a split second, her eyes looked like G's did when he was waiting on her to wake up. She looked at Suave with nothing in her eyes.

"Tell me when, the bitch dead to me anyway." Shadow looked at me.

"These mother fuckers crazy." I mouthed to his ass and we laughed at our silent joke.

"Can we go to the house now, a nigga balls sticking to my damn thighs?"

"Yeah, but it has to be quick. We have to stay here until she gets out. We can rotate." Suave stated as we got ready to leave. "Baby bro, you coming?'

"I'm not leaving until she leaves."

"Nigga you gone smell like death and booty. Just know you ain't getting in my car. You better ask my mama how I feel about that funky shit."

"Shut your dumb ass up and come on." Suave pushed my ass out the door and we headed to the main house.

The emotions were high there when we walked in and I knew everybody was scared. Reality set in that it's a chance all our ass wasn't coming back. Not me though, I died already fuck that. It's somebody else turn. After explaining everything to the entire house, I went up to my room to wash my ass.

"Baby, I don't like this shit. What if you don't come back?"

"Your ass better not fuck nobody else for five years. Make sure a nigga really gone this time."

"This is not the time to play, I'm dead ass. It could have been any one of you laid up in that bed."

"I know that, but one thing is for certain if we don't go all of our ass might be die. This has to be done. I'm not going nowhere. Just keep our baby girl safe no matter what." Pulling her into the bathroom with me, we got in the shower together. They can say what they want, but I was about to get this pussy.

****

It's been a long three weeks and the shit had been wearing everybody down, but they were finally releasing Paradise. A nigga was tired of hospital rooms and I couldn't wait to get her ass home. Paris was at the house getting it together because we were throwing her a welcome home party. This would be the last gathering we had before our ass had to go to Columbia.

The trip was in two days and I couldn't wait to get this shit over with. We had been bringing G clothes and he showered at the hospital, I couldn't let my man go out like that. His ass was walking around smelling like peeled lips. After loading Paradise up in the car, we headed to the house. Baby Face was finally healed all the way and I wondered if she was gone be good to take this trip. If we waited any longer, the old bitch was gone have time to build an entire army. Hoping she was good to go, I pushed those thoughts in the back of my mind and prepared to have a drama free day. We all needed this shit and I couldn't wait to get some real food in my fucking system.

Pulling up to the house, I prayed these niggas knew how to take a surprise. They didn't come across as the type that had people jumping out from behind places with the light off. Fuck around and the entire house be dead as fuck. That's why I told they ass just hang banners and everybody just kick it and have a good time. We not doing that surprise bullshit.

As soon as she walked in the door and saw the decorations and shit, her hard demeanor and walls came down. She looked happy as fuck to see everybody and I was glad. As long as Paradise was happy, G was too. Tank and Suave looked like they were ready to fuck in the front room and I had to remind they ass I ain't play that shit. Reaching over to them, I flicked that Bic and he put her down.

"Damn nigga I get it with your cock blocking ass. You don't want nobody to get pussy but you."

"Damn right, now go party." Face was in the corner texting and I walked over.

"Nigga fuck you doing?"

"This new chick I been dating trying to see me and I was debating on whether or not to let her come over here. A nigga need some pussy, but you know we don't bring outsiders to the house."

"With everything that's going on and the war that's coming, let her come. Shid, it might be the last time our ass get to dig in some guts. You think Shay gone be pissed? I saw her ass walking like she had on a ten dollar pair of heels and them bitches was leaning?"

"She got a nigga and I don't do drama."

"Cool, then invite her ass over." Walking to the table, I grabbed me a plate and sat down to eat. My plate was piled up with baked beans and deviled eggs and I felt sorry for whoever sat next to my ass. Everything was going smooth and this was a perfect moment. Until my mama got her nasty ass up and started grinding on the pastor. He was standing his ass there grinning and shit. When she dropped down to the ground I was ready to snatch her ass up.

"Let mama be great. Yall been through a lot these last couple of weeks. She need this." Looking over at Paris, I nodded my head and kept eating. She was right. We had the right to get loose. Once I was done eating, a nigga laid back and just watched my family have a good time. Shit was going good until my stomach started boiling. Glancing over at Paris, I saw she was sleep and I lifted my leg and passed gas. That shit felt good, but it smelt like horse shit and eggs.

After the third time doing it, I was glad nobody had come my way and smelled this shit. Feeling like I would be good to go if I let loose one last time, I lifted that leg and let it ride. Paris jumped out of her sleep and her head whipped around so fast, I started laughing before she said anything.

"Blaze if you open yo ass one more time, imma fuck you up."

"My bad, it's them damn beans." She rolled her eyes and laid back down, I couldn't do shit, but laugh. Face walked to the middle of the floor with this fine ass bitch and everybody stopped to look.

"Hey yall, this my friend Royalty." She waved and we all spoke.

"Who the fuck is this you done brought in our shit? Your ass was ready to throw my dick out the doe, but you come walking in here with some white pussy."

"Ma, she not white."

"Is she black? Then her ass is white. You got a lot of nerve I should fuck Devon right here on your couch to teach your ass not to fuck with me."

"Ma, for once can you be normal."

"For once can you suck deez nuts? I ain't think so." She walked off mumbling and I laughed hard as hell. She had a point though, but she ain't gotta be so damn ignorant." Like we were some kids, all the men gathered around as if she was a new toy

Face got for Christmas. Smalls walked up with two plates in his hand.

"Am I tripping or do she look like Journey." Gangsta and Suave looked at Paradise and then back to her. They looked at each other and both of them pulled their guns on Royalty.

"Party over everybody get the fuck out." Me and my brothers were lost as hell. Who in the fuck is Journey?

CHAPTER 29- SUAVE

When Baby Face introduced Royalty, I hadn't really paid attention to her looks. My bitch was the baddest in the room if you asked me. When Smalls walked up and said that shit, I actually got a good look at her. Her and Journey looked so much alike, it was creepy. Looking over at Paradise, you could see the resemblance to her as well. Knowing there was no way this shit could be a coincidence especially since we know Paradise's mother was behind it, we raised our guns on the bitch.

Blaze and them were looking confused, but they would figure it out soon. Staring into Royalty's eyes, she tried to keep a straight face, but her eyes changed over. Not to mention, any other bitch would have been scared and screaming. She stood there saying nothing.

"Party over. Everybody get the fuck out." Gangsta wasn't playing no games and I wasn't either.

"Wait, yall know her?"

"Naw, we never met the bitch but we know who she is. Tell him who you are." The bitch didn't flinch or mumble a word. Waiting until everybody had cleared out of the room, I hit her in the face with my gun. Paradise walked over and looked at her, reaching in her pocket she pulled out her wallet. Passing us the ID, we were right, but I knew that anyway my gut was never wrong.

"Royalty Garzon. This bitch."

"We know yall get it, but help us figure out what the fuck is going on." Baby Face was getting pissed, he didn't like being out of the loop.

"Her name is Paradise Garzon." Waiting on them to catch on, I continued. "A couple years ago, Paradise's father sent his daughter Journey in to set up G. Nobody knew they were sisters but him. Tank killed her and we went to war with the Garzon Cartel. The same Cartel we are at war at right now.

When Smalls said she looked like Journey, we knew it was no way that shit was coincidence with everything that's going on."

"I wonder how many kids that old ass nigga got." Smalls said while he was smacking on some chicken.

"I don't know, but when this bitch wakes up we gone get everything we need out of her ass. Face go set up the basement. We need every tool and knife you have in this mother fucker. Shadow, carry her downstairs."

After everything was set up, we waited on her to wake up. When she finally opened her eyes, you could see she knew it was over for her.

"Did you know about me?" Paradise started the questioning off.

"Fuck you." She spit in Paradise face and by the looks on the Hoover brother's faces, I knew they had no idea Paradise was worse than G. They were looking too calm. She walked over to the table and grabbed a knife, in one swift motion, she sliced her ear off.

"Did you know about me?"

"Hey sis, not to bother you or anything while you in here cutting up bodies, but you did slice her ear off how she gone hear you?" Paradise gave Blaze a death stare and he laughed and backed back.

"My bad, you can continue. I'm just saying you mad she ain't responding but you stepping on her ear." This wasn't the time to be joking, but I swear I couldn't stop laughing. It was the truth. Grabbing a meat tenderizer, Paradise hit her in the face with it, tearing off her skin.

"Bitch your mama sent you here to die. She knew you wouldn't make it out. I'm guessing she didn't tell you about us, the stories and how we get down. You gone sit here and protect a mother fucker that set you up to die?"

"Yeah, I knew about you and I didn't give a fuck. Growing up all I heard was I needed to be more like Paradise, but look at you. Bitch you're a fucking mom and I'm next in line to be the heiress to the Garzon Cartel."

"I'm sure they need a mother fucker that can hear in charge." Looking at Blaze, he threw his hands up and laughed.

"Let me talk to her sis." Moving Paradise back, I walked over to Royalty.

"You don't have to say anything, I just need you to nod. Do you know who I am?" She shook her head yes.

"Then you know what I am about. I won't sit here and threaten you or raise my voice. You should already know what's coming if you don't answer my questions. How many men do your mom have in Columbia?" She looked, but didn't respond. Pulling a chair up, I sat down.

"Smalls, go find me a dog."

"Nigga where am I supposed to go find a dog?"

"I don't care if you have to steal one out somebody yard, just come back with me a dog."

"Sick ass nigga. Bitch just answer the damn question. Do you know what he about to do to your ass?" When she didn't respond, he left out. Never breaking my stare, I waited for Smalls to come back.

****

He walked in the door with a Pitbull and threw him on the ground. Standing up, I rolled my sleeves up and walked over to the table. Grabbing a butcher knife, I headed back to her. Leaning down, I whispered in the dog's ear and stood up.

"Suave, you not gone ask her again and give her a chance?" Turning to Face, I smirked.

"I don't give second chances." Before anybody saw it coming, I chopped her arm off to the elbow. Throwing it to the dog, he didn't move.

"Eat." The dog started tearing her arm to shreds. Royalty was screaming for dear life and the shit didn't move me.

"How many men do your mom have?"

"Not many, yall took a lot of them out. She is regrouping and plan on coming here in two days. They plan to take your entire family out. Now please, let me go." Bringing the knife down on her other arm, I threw it to the dog.

"Eat." The screams got louder, but she had no idea what was about to happen to her.

"G, you want a part of this before I end her?"

"Come here Shadow." The Hoover brothers were looking worried because they knew baby brother wasn't about this life. "Take this brick and bam her head in until that shit is removed from her body. You are not allowed to stop until you have a head

to give me. Do you understand?'

"Naw G, he not ready for that." Baby Face wasn't with the

shit G was on, but he had to learn at some point.

"Do you understand." G never took his eyes off Shadow.

He grabbed the brick from Gangsta and kicked her chair back.

Slamming the brick down, he kept hitting her until her head

snapped off. Grabbing the head, he threw it at Blaze.

"Nigga don't play with me, I'll set your asshole on fire."

When Shadow walked back over, he had a different look in his

eye. He may have had a beast in him all along and no one knew it.

"Paradise and G, grab a knife. It's time to make her ass

disappear. Yall can go upstairs if you don't want to see this. It's

about to get messy. We'll put her out back for you to play with

Blaze. Get your lighter ready." Everybody headed out, but

Shadow.

"What we gotta do?"

CHAPTER 30- BABY FACE

"Who the fuck yall done let in our house? These mother fuckers are sick as hell." Quick was trying not to throw up.

"The devil. I admit their way of killing is intense but it's effective. I'm worried about Shadow. I think he is trying to prove to G he ain't a bitch, but he biting off more than he can chew."

"The dog too. How Suave ass gone make that mutt eat the bitch arm in her face." I laughed at Blaze.

"Nigga you know how they get down, I'm surprised you acting shocked."

"Knowing it and seeing it is two different things. I'm just ready to light some shit up, I hope it don't take them long I'm trying to get some pussy."

"Nigga you do realize they about to cut that girl body up and hand it to your ass right?"

"And I'm gone hand her ass over to hell." We laughed at this nigga and walked up the stairs. He talking about them, but the fact that he don't see nothing wrong with the shit he do lets me know he just as crazy. We rounded the corner and Juicy was sitting there on the couch. Not moving, I just looked at her. She looked so broken and I wanted to wrap her in my arms, but I stood still.

"Damn sis, you must have smelled your dick in jeopardy and where your ass been? You look bad girl. Look like your ass been sleeping under the porch." Punching Blaze in his arm, I needed him to shut the fuck up.

"Can I talk to you Face?"

"Now you want to talk?"

"Please." Not having the heart to treat her how she did me, I walked over. My brothers went towards the kitchen and I looked at her waiting for her to speak.

"I'm sorry for the way I was acting. I have PPD."

"Don't bring that shit to my brother with your nasty ass. Face you better get checked out ain't no telling how long she had that shit. You ain't want me to set you on fire, but you been burning all this time." Looking over at Blaze, he had eased back in the front room.

"Nigga that mean Postpartum Depression. Get your dumb ass out of here and let us talk.

"Wait, so her pussy depressed? Nigga just fuck her and get your girl back. Cus your new bitch getting cut to pieces right now. Her pussy definitely gone be WOE." Running my hand down my face in frustration, I was ready to beat his ass. "Aight, I'm gone. Niggas never want my opinion and shit. Fuck yall."

Watching the doorway until he left, I turned and faced Juicy again.

"Why didn't you tell me?" The tears started falling down her face.

"I didn't know what was wrong with me. All I knew is the baby and you were too much to deal with so I left. You don't know how many nights I cried myself to sleep and I just needed to get away. When I tried to kill myself, my mama took me to the hospital and they told me what was wrong with me.

I'm in therapy now and I would like it if you come with me and we work on our family. If you don't want to, I understand but I had to come tell you what was going on. I'm sorry Face, I really do love you." Grabbing her, I pulled her into my chest.

"I'll go, but not until I get back."

"You going to see your new bitch?"

"Naw she down there in the basement getting ate up by a dog." Looking at me like I was crazy, she waited for me to explain. "Go upstairs and take a shower and lay down. When we done with this shit, I'll tell you everything. I'm glad you're back." Even though she still looked bad, her face brightened up. It was going to be a long road, but I was here for it.

"I'm guessing we done fucking now since your wife back." Turning my head, Shay was standing there in some booty shorts and a sports bra. She was looking fine as fuck and I needed Tsunami to sit the fuck down.

"Yeah, we gone try to work our shit out. You good though?" My mouth was saying no, but my dick was saying blow that bitch back out now. She needed to be good because I ain't want no problems or drama. We had enough shit going on. She walked over to me and rubbed Tsunami.

"At least I know somebody still wants me. If you ever want to hook up again, you know how to get in touch." She slid her tongue in my mouth while she caressed my dick. When she walked off, I wanted so bad to follow up behind her and go for one last ride before I got back on track with my family.

Knowing that shit wouldn't be in my best interest, I stayed my ass put. God himself had to come hold me back because my dick was trying his best to pull me towards her.

"Damn nigga, you got three hoes under the same roof. Juicy gone kill your ass." Walking towards Blaze to beat his ass, he took off running. "Nigga wait until your dick go down first. Your ass wanna wrestle and your shit looking like it's ready to bust through your pants."

Looking down, my shit was at full attention. Laughing, I tried to readjust my shit before Juicy really did beat my ass. Walking out in the yard, they had just finished putting all of Royalty's remains in the garbage.

"Go head Blaze, do your thang." This nigga actually smiled because it was his turn and he got to do the finale. After everything was cleaned up, we walked back in the house.

"We have to leave tomorrow. We can't give her the chance to fully regroup and come here. Smalls you and your crew should stay behind that way somebody is here that can protect our family."

"Hold the fuck up, you know Drea's pussy is friendly. I ain't leaving his ass here to run all through my girl pussy while I'm over there trying not to die again."

"SHUT UP BLAZE." Everybody screamed at the same time.

"We leave at six, everybody go and get some rest. Fuck your girls, love on your kids, and make sure you stay alert. See yall in the morning." We all went our separate ways and I headed upstairs to my room. Walking down the hall, I heard some noises coming out of one of the guest rooms. Sticking my head in to make sure everything was good, Shay was laying on the bed asshole naked playing with her pussy. When she realized I was watching, she really got worked up. Her moans had Tsunami back at attention. Watching until she was finished, I walked over to her and slid my hand up her pussy. The shit was so wet, I wanted to dive in so bad. Sticking my finger in her mouth, she sucked my shit so good I almost put my dick in it.

"If I wasn't a good nigga, I'll have my dick in your cervix right now. This shit is done baby girl. It was one night and it's over. Get some sleep, we got a long day tomorrow. Kissing her on her cheek, I walked out of her room. Heading to my room with a swollen dick, I knew I was gone be in the shower beating my meat. Juicy ain't gave me none in forever. Not even attempting to get in the bed with her, I needed to release this nut.

As soon as the water hit my body, I started stroking my shit. Feeling another hand wrap around my dick, I knew I was about to lose this battle. Shay was determined to get this dick and I didn't have the restraint to say no anymore. My dick was so hard the shit was aching. Turning around, I came face to face with Juicy. Picking her up, I slid her down on my dick fast and hard.

CHAPTER 31- QUICK

All these niggas crazy. Now don't get me wrong, I have no

problem laying a nigga down. I've been killing all my life, but this

shit was on a different level. Growing up, I always thought mother

fuckers were exaggerating the stories about G and them. You know

how niggas in the hood do, but I have witnessed this shit first hand

and my ass was sick to my stomach. I always thought Blaze could

get a check for the shit he did and how he didn't mind cooking a

nigga. This was different level type shit.

Heading upstairs, I needed to gather my thoughts for

tomorrow. Seeing Shadow do that shit to ol girl was fucking with

my mind. Not the action itself, but how easy it was for G to get

him to do it. We always protected him from the worst part of this

street shit. He was the baby and it was just certain shit we didn't

want him doing. Hell, when we were robbing banks, we always left

the nigga in the car. I couldn't wait for this shit to be over, it was

getting way out of hand and I just wanted things to get back to

normal.

Walking in the kids room, Zavi was sleep and I hugged and kissed him. I hated that he saw another nigga and looked to him as another daddy. Yeah, I killed his ass but my son grieving him pissed me off. Walking out the room, I headed to mine and got in the shower. A nigga had too much on his dome and just wanted to take my ass to sleep.

"You okay Quick?"

"Yeah ma, I'm good. Get some rest, when you wake up I'll be gone. We heading out at six." The tears started forming in her eyes and I felt bad.

"Please be safe, I can't lose you we just found our way back to each other."

"It's going to be okay. Once we are done here, we are done for good."

"How do you know it won't be somebody else that will pop up and then you have to go to war with them. Is it ever really over? Can a person ever fully retire?"

"I don't know the answer to that, but I will say this. The Hoover Gang is strong enough to handle whatever comes our way.

You just gotta have faith in your man and his abilities. I'll always protect my family no matter what is thrown our way. We got out the game, but I don't know if someone will try us again. That's what this street life is about. You knew the type of nigga you were marrying and you have to be strong enough to deal with that.

Look at Paradise and Tank. Now I'm not asking you to be a killer, but they don't question they man or his abilities. They have full trust that they gone handle the shit. I need you to be strong and know that I'm gone be good. Anything can happen, but if it does you can't break. We have a son with a baby on the way. They will need you. Do you understand what I am saying to you?" She nodded her head and I kissed her.

"A nigga need to take a shower and get some sleep. Come with me, this dick ain't gone suck itself." Slapping me in the head, she laughed as she got up. Tomorrow would be hell, but tonight I was gone lose myself in this pussy. Ash and the kids were my everything and I was gone fight like hell to get back to them. Even if I had to cut a bitch arm off. Laughing at them sick niggas, I closed my eyes as her mouth wrapped around my dick. I definitely

had to come back to this shit.

****

"So what's the plan?" Nobody has said anything about how

we were going to handle this.

"Since Paradise know the entire layout of the compound we

are allowing her to take the lead. If any of you see her mother, hold

her until she gets there. Nobody is to be left alone, keep your eyes

and your ears open. Quick you and G are going in the front since

you are our most precise shooters. Take down the wall of defense

and we will cover you." Baby Face barked orders and we all

listened.

"Tank and her crew will take the back. Blaze, wait what the

fuck you doing with that?" We turned around and this nigga had

his big ass flame thrower on his back.

"Nigga it's about to be the fourth of July in this bitch. That

lil ass lighter wasn't gone do the trick. Yall cut em down, I'm gone

light they ass up. Simple. Now hurry up with this long ass lecture. I

swear you and Suave will have a nigga sitting there for hours for one damn plan. All your ugly ass had to say was shoot until ain't

shit moving. The end. Let's go shit. Yall got this nigga Smalls at

home with my bitch. If she even thinks my ass dead issa slip."

"Let's go, this nigga is losing his mind. G you ready?"

Looking over at Gangsta this nigga's eyes were empty as hell. He

didn't even respond, nigga jumped the gate and started shooting.

"Fuck, hurry up and get in there. This nigga crazy." I

agreed with Suave as I leaped over and covered G. We were laying

niggas down and it wasn't long before you heard gun fire going off

everywhere. I covered the niggas on the ground while he took out

the niggas on the roof. When we walked inside, it was too quiet.

"Turn your back to me. You keep that side covered and I

got this side." Me and G went back to back. As the guards started

pouring in, we laid they ass out. My ass almost pissed myself when

Blaze rounded the corner shooting fire. Having a flash back, I got

the fuck out the way before that shit hit me. Knowing it wouldn't

be long before the house was up in flames, we made our way

through the rest of the big ass house.

"Damn, how many rooms this bitch got?" Me and Blaze

laughed, but G didn't crack a smile. After walking the entire house,

G decided to split up.

"I need to find Paradise and this bitch. Yall go outside and

make sure the others are good."

"You sure?" He gave me a look that let me know he was

straight. Walking outside, we rounded the compound and it was

good to see Tank and her crew was good. They had cleared the

entire back yard.

"Where is Shadow, Suave, and Paradise?"

"We don't know, we thought they went in with yall."

Walking off, I noticed some people in a room. Creeping up to the

window, Paradise had her gun pointed at her mom. Noticing some

kind of trigger in her hand, me and Blaze looked at each other.

"This bitch the real Blaze. She about to blow all our ass to

Hell." What the fuck have we gotten ourselves into?"

CHAPTER 32- PARADISE

As soon as the outside was clear, I entered the house. I saw

my momma rounding the corner and rushed behind her. Walking

into her office, she stood by the window behind her desk.

"You were always such a disappointment. No matter what

you did, I could never get Louis to see you weren't the child he

thought you was. He had more faith in you than he had in me his

own fucking wife. Did you know, I stood right here in this house

and watched you kill your father. He would have given you the

world, but it was nothing for you to betray him for that gutter rat.

All is well that ends well though, you saved me from

having to do it. He was becoming weak. The enemy was creeping

in taking over and all he cared about was bringing you back home.

He wasn't here for months and I had to run shit and clean up his

mess. You're weak just like he is because that low life means more

to you than anything else."

"You were always jealous of me and that's okay. I found a

family who loves and accept me just as I was. I killed your

husband because he was weak. I killed your bitch ass daughter

because she was weak. Garzon's don't do weak. Did you know

jealousy is an emotion and emotions are weak? You know what

that means right? It's time to send your bitch ass to your husband."

"I don't think so." She lifted her hand and I could see she

was holding a trigger. "If I put my hand on this button, we all go.

Are you willing to kill your low life as well since you just took a

bullet for him?" As soon as she said that, G, Suave, and Shadow

entered the room.

"Why haven't you killed her yet?" G was looking at me as

if he was unsure I could do the job.

"Because she wants to save your life." She dangled the

trigger around. "Now, everybody put their guns down and let me

walk out of here. If not, we all go." We all looked at each other and

knew we were in a catch twenty two. If she walked out of here, she

would kill us all and if we didn't put the guns down, we all die.

Not really having a choice, we got ready to lower our weapons

when a stream of fire came through the window. This nigga Blaze

was torching her from outside the window. Quick came right

behind him and shot the trigger out of her hand. Wanting to be the one that caused her to take her last breath, I walked up to her burning body and emptied my clip in her head. Grabbing the fire extinguisher off the wall, I put the fire out. Looking over at Gangsta, I smiled.

"Hey G, you want to make a bet."

CHAPTER 33- BLAZE

We were finally back home and I couldn't be happier. The shit was done and my family made it out one last time on top. When paradise put the fire out, I was pissed. I wanted to see that bitch body turn to ashes. She turned to G and was smiling all goofy and shit.

"Hey G, you want to make a bet." When he started smiling back, me and my brothers looked at each other trying to figure out what the fuck was going on.

"This time, loser has to do everything dealing with Kenya bad ass for two months. Feeding, cleaning, babysitting the works."

"Bet."

"The fuck are you niggas talking about?" Suave pulled us out of the room laughing.

"You don't want to be in there for that. When they first met, they made a bet to see who could cut our parents up the smallest and fastest. Nastiest shit I ever seen. Let's go, let them have they moment."

"Nigga and you feeding a bitch to a dog wasn't nasty? All you niggas sick." We laughed as we waited outside for the nasty ass couple to finish. Them niggas was made for each other.

As much as we wanted they creepy ass to go back where the fuck they came from, watching them in the lobby with their bags didn't feel right.

"Shadow's birthday is tomorrow. Stay one more day and let us take yall out to thank yall."

"One more day nigga and we better have fun. I been dodging bullets and killing since I been here." Laughing at Suave, we all went upstairs to get ready. Out of everything we been through this month, I was more excited about this than anything. We hadn't been out in a year and I couldn't wait to party.

Throwing on my all black Gucci button up, black Gucci jeans, and my red high top Giuseppe's, I was ready to go. When we all made it down to the foyer, everybody looked like money. It was almost a billion dollars standing in this foyer and that right there was enough for me to be happy. Can't complain about the life we chose to live or the ups and downs that came with it. At the end of the day, we came out on top and lived to tell the story. Jumping in our Phantoms, G rode with me and Suave rode with Face.

As soon as we pulled up to Hoover Nights, I started smiling.

"Nigga, what the fuck you smiling at?"

"You have no idea. Watch this shit." When the first set of headlights went off the crowd went nuts. G looked at me all confused.

"What the fuck they screaming for?" Not responding, I just laughed and turned my lights off. Opening our door at the same time, we stepped out. G and Suave stepped out as well and we walked to their side. The crowd was going crazy and people recognized who they were.

"Oh my God, Lucifer. Can I just touch your hand?" One of the girls screamed from the crowd.

"What kind of place is this?" Me and my brothers looked at each other and started doing our wave. The crowd joined in and started chanting.

"HOOVER. HOOVER. HOOVER." Suave was laughing, but G ass had to ruin our moment.

"Yall aggy as hell. If yall don't bring yall dumb ass on. I need a fucking drink and you out here waving and shit at the crowd like you the queen of England." Laughing, we all walked in the club. Of course, the crowd went nuts when they saw us.

"Awww shit, The Hoover Gang in the mother fucking building. Wait, did these niggas get Suave and Lucifer to come out and party with us. I need everybody to raise they fucking glasses and salute some real niggas. You in the presence of Legends." Everybody raised their cups as our song played.

"I think I'm Big Meech, Larry Hoover. Whipping work, hallelujah. One nation, under God real niggas getting money from the fucking start." BMF by Rick Ross played over the speakers as we partied with the crowd.

This was the life and I wouldn't apologize for nothing we had done. It made us who we are today and we some boss ass niggas with some bad bitches to hold us down. More money than we knew what to do with, how the fuck can you complain behind some shit like that? We had made it and we defeated all our

enemies. Drea hadn't slipped on anymore dicks so life was great.

We didn't have shit else to worry about and we could just live life

how we wanted. Shadow came and stood by Gangsta and I didn't

think shit of it until I heard him try to whisper.

"G, will you train me?"

THE END...

Message from the Hoover Gang....

Thank you so much for rocking with us for four books

strong. You have made us one of the biggest series this summer.

We hate to go, but whenever you're missing a real nigga just reach

in your pocket and flick your Bic. Everybody good over here.

Mama and the pastor getting married, Quick and Ash had they

baby girl and Shadow dick finally work. Kimmie is pregnant. Blaze

still lighting shit up and Baby Face and Juicy worked out their

problems. We go visit Gangsta and Suave often. We are going to

miss you and we appreciate all of your support. Grab you some paperbacks so you can always have a piece of us in your life. We

love you.

TURN THE PAGE FOR ANNOUNCEMENTS AND A SNEAK

PEEK.

I GOTTA BE THE ONE YOU LOVE

A STAND ALONE NOVEL

PROLOGUE

I can hear movement in the hallway as I lay in my room scared shitless. I got up and turned everything off so that anyone walking pass my room would assume I was asleep. I tried my best not to make a sound or any movements for fear that they would hear me. God please help me.

The footsteps got closer and closer to my bedroom door. I wanted to hide and pretend I wasn't there, but I didn't want my mom to think I snuck out of the house. As I heard the door knob turn all I could do was pray it was over quickly.

CHAPTER ONE

KIRA

Every girl dreams of a romance like the ones we see on tv, but in reality, that shit doesn't exist. At least not for me. My name is Kirana Mosely, but everybody calls me Kira. I am sixteen years old and technically I am a virgin, even though other people would beg to differ. Most people describe me as mysterious because of my look, but mostly because of my quiet demeanor. I am 5'7 with really long curly hair. I am a light brown complexion, but it looks as if I'm mixed with something. Rumor has it around the family that my mama was already pregnant with me when she met my daddy and put it off on him as if he was the father. My mama is a milk chocolate complexion and my daddy is midnight black. I don't really look like either of them. I have a petite frame but my breast and my butt was a nice size for my weight. I would probably look amazing if I had nice clothes to show it off, but I don't. We live in the West Suburbs of Chicago in a town called Hillside. My mama never worked she was always at home taking care of the house and catering to my daddy's every need. My dad worked on the railroad, but was laid off so money has been tight for the past three years. They always tell me there wasn't enough money left over for me to get new clothes and shoes, but it always seemed to be enough for mama's cigarettes and daddy's liquor. My cousin Dee lived down the street from me. Her mama and my mama was sister's. They weren't rich, but they had more than we had, so Dee snuck me some of her clothes here and there. She was literally the only person I talked to. Everyone else treated me like a dirty bum as if it was contagious. I was grateful for the barely worn Air Force one's Dee had given me as I looked down at my feet while I waited on her to come out the house. She finally walked out the door.

"Damn bitch it took you long enough I was about to walk off on your ass." She walked towards me doing her model walk.

"Hoe you know it takes time to get this cute." I must admit she was really cute. She was 5'6 and thick as hell. She had her hair cut in a bob and she stayed rocking all the newest name brand clothes and shoes.

"Girl if it takes that long to get cute you aint that cute." We laughed as we walked to the school. This was our last month of school for the year so I didn't want to be late to any of my classes because I needed to get all A's. I was trying to get a

scholarship so I can get the fuck out of my parent's house. I

really hated being there and I was determined to get out one way

or another. As we walked in the door all the kids were standing

in the hallway. And just like a snow ball on a hot summer day

there he was. Tremaine Donaldson, but everyone called him Tre.

He was the finest boy in school and the most popular. Not to

mention, the star of the basketball team. Everyone knew that he

was going to play pro ball. Hell, he could play in the NBA right

now if it was allowed. He was just that good. He stood 6'3 and

had a very muscular build. He kept his hair cut low, but wavy.

He had a baby face, and was a milk chocolate complexion that

would definitely melt in your mouth and not in your hands. He

turned and looked at me and I swear my panties instantly got wet.

My cousin Dee wanted him as well, but nobody wanted him like

me. I dreamed of him almost every night. I don't know if you

believe in love at first sight, but it was just that for me.

   I wanted him deep in my soul, but I knew that he would

never be with a girl like me. He had the looks, the money, and

could have any girl he possibly wanted. Why the fuck would he want a bum like me? So I dated him in my dreams and I was

okay with that. As soon as we approached them, Dee turned on

her charm.

"Hey baby you been looking for me?" He showed his

pearly whites as he responded.

"Girl you don't want me. Your ass always playing." He

gave her a hug and him and his boys walked off. She turned to

me fanning herself.

"Girl I would fuck him right here on this mother fucking

floor." Although I would never admit it and especially out loud, I

would definitely give him some.

"I think every girl in this school would Dee." She shook

her head in agreement as we went our separate ways to class. My

first period was English and I shared it with Tre. I had a full

forty five minutes to look at him and daydream every day. The

teacher started to speak.

"Okay class, final exams are coming up. We are going to

pair up two students to do the assignment. You will have to write

an essay on violence in the community. The assignment is worth

60% of your final grades. Both of you will be graded equally. To make it fair I have put one side of the class names in a jar and the other half of the class will pull one. As I call your name come up and pull your partner." This shit was about to blow me because I didn't like talking to anyone or really being around people. They didn't like me and I didn't care for them. Half of them was dumb anyway and I would have to carry they ass.

"Kirana come pull a name please." I walked up to the teacher's desk, smacking my teeth, and pulled a piece of paper out. Rolling my eyes as I opened the paper, I could not believe my fucking eyes. I had pulled Tre's name. I was freaking out because I didn't know how he would react to being my partner. I walked over to him hoping he didn't embarrass the shit out of my ass in front of everybody.

"Hey, looks like you are stuck with me on the assignment." He looked up at me with his perfect face and smiled.

"Good if I'm going to be hooked up I would rather it be with the smartest girl in the school." Of course, my insides

melted as he continued to talk. "Let's exchange numbers so we

can link up after school."

"I don't have a cell phone." I said embarrassed.

"It's okay we will figure it out. Let me write my number

down in the meantime, and you can call me when you get around

a phone until we can get something worked out." He wrote his

number down on a piece of paper for me and it made me feel

small. People didn't write numbers down anymore, everyone had

cell phones these days. You could just pull your shit out and type

it in. He handed me the paper.

"Meet me at my locker after school." I nodded my head

and floated off. I swear I felt like the luckiest bitch to ever walk

these halls. I get to be around Tre every single day after school.

Even though I know he didn't look at me like that I couldn't wait

to be around him.

****

The end of the day couldn't come fast enough. When the

last bell sounded I grabbed my shit so fast and hurried to his locker. He was with his friends and Dee and her friends was close by. When I approached him, his friend Jeremy spoke up.

"What the fuck are you lost or something? The bum bitches section is over there." The entire hallway started laughing. I froze in my tracks. I wanted to say something, but no words would come out. So, I did what I do best, I ran. As I made my wait out the door tearing the little sole I had left on my shoes, I could hear Dee going off on the boy about fucking with her cousin. I didn't stay to see the outcome I just wanted to get far away from there. Now don't get me wrong I could fight my ass off, but I was not about to sit around and be the butt of everyone's joke.

KEEPING UP WITH LATOYA NICOLE

FB: Latoya Nicole Williams

Ig: Latoyanicole35

Twitter: Latoyanicole35

SC: iamTOYS

Email: latoyanicole@yahoo.com

Join my readers group on fb: Toy's House of Books.

OTHER BOOKS BY LATOYA NICOLE

NO WAY OUT: MEMOIRS OF A HUSTLA'S GIRL

NO WAY OUT 2: RETURN OF A SAVAGE

GANGSTA'S PARADISE

GANGSTA'S PARADISE 2: HOW DEEP IS YOUR LOVE

ADDICTED TO HIS PAIN (A STANDALONE NOVEL)

LOVE AND WAR: A HOOVER GANG AFFAIR 1-3

COMING SOON...

RELEASING SEPT 26TH I GOTTA BE THE ONE YOU LOVE

(STANDALONE)

CREEPING WITH THE ENEMY 2: A SAVAGE STOLE MY

HEART.

CPSIA information can be obtained
at www.ICGtesting.com
Printed in the USA
LVHW05s1945200618
581394LV00021B/366/P